The Two Secrets

By

Sarah Jane Gross

Original artwork by Sarah Jane Gross

Author's Note:

While this book is largely fictitious,
I do pay tribute to family members
long gone, who we loved and cherished.

Table of Contents

Chapter 1
The Featherwins
Marshfield, Coos County, Oregon, circa 1920

The rain was coming down hard in Marshfield in Coos County, southern Oregon. Betty Featherwin thought with a wistful sigh how the heavy rain, growing more torrid with each clap of thunder, would cause a troublesome puddle where the ground dipped by the porch. And the key seemed to stick in the rusted door whenever the wood contracted from the damp in the air. No matter, for she was quite accustomed to these rain-filled days, which were frequent in this part of the state. Marshfield had become a bustling shipping and lumber town over the past decade, and no amount of rain would stop the mill from running or the men from putting in a day's work.

As she continued to gaze out the window in the parlor of her mother's home, Betty smiled. The rain would neither stop her, as she fully intended to attend to her daily duties in town. The clock had not struck the nine-o-clock hour, and so it was early yet. She could hear the clatter of pots and pans just down the hall in the kitchen—the heart and center of the home—and the faint scent of bread as her mother, Bea, warmed a loaf in the oven. Bea would be baking again, trying her hand at an old family recipe. Last week, it was blueberry-lavender scones. This morning, by the smells beginning to waft through the house, it could be pastries with strawberry, lemon, and cream. Even now, Betty could hear what sounded like a whisk and a splash of milk. While the house was spread out, just one level, the design was open and one room spilled into the next. It was always rather cool and echoey, with planks of myrtle wood on the floors and every table top. Thus, it was rather easy to hear sounds and voices in the kitchen while one sat in the front parlor. It was also rather usual to smell herbs, spices, and confections with Bea cooking often and the smell eventually reaching every room of the house. Betty shook her head fondly. She suspected that Bea's frequent baking had more to do with outcompeting Mrs. Highley, their neighbor; though everyone knew that Mrs. Highley's was the place to go for the best refreshments.

Beatrice Featherwin—or Bea, as she was called—had lived in Marshfield for the past 20 years, having moved from Missouri after she met her husband, Henry. Betty, their only child, was now a blooming young woman of 20, with a vibrant spirit and a hint of rose on her cheeks. Bea wanted her to settle down and marry, and was admittedly a little shocked and embarrassed at Betty's notions of working and spending so many days wandering alone at the shore and lumbermill. Betty swore that she was not alone, and that she always had a cat or two for companionship anyway (there was a multitude of stray cats down around the mill). Bea did not quite believe her. Betty was so full of fancies and ideas that it was hard for Bea to know if what she said was true or just borne of her imagination. Betty had always been an imaginative and precocious person, loving stories and fairy tales when she was a child and spending much of her time with her father, Henry, in his bookshop. It was a quaint shop at the edge of town, popular for its eclectic collection of letters, books, and manuscripts and for its views of the sea. Henry would take Betty on a Saturday and wile away the hours re-telling tales and fables, entertaining his daughter and the locals who stopped in too. It was fun for Betty, of course, though Bea doubted that it was at all educational. Little did she know then that Betty would one day manage that bookshop.

When Henry first opened it, some eighteen years ago,

many folks liked to come in and just shoot the breeze with him as he shared stories of the lumbermill. Henry still worked at the North Bend Mill & Lumber Company as a laborer then, and had made many local friends. He had worked in the mill back in Missouri before coming here to Oregon, where, in the early years of this 20th century, demand for wood and shipbuilding material was at its height. After a couple of years with North Bend Mill & Lumber, he took a turn as lighthouse keeper for a change of pace.

Once he learned that he would have a daughter, however, he refocused his efforts on his wife, Bea, and providing for his family. He made a good living at the mill and became friends with the young men who worked there too. Good, strong men who did not mind hard labor and who drew their energy from the earth and the sea. Many of these men's families had occupied Coos County for decades and held Coos Indian blood in their veins. For them, the manual work with lumber and the feel of natural materials in their hands was an inherent part of who they were and had immense value. Henry listened to their stories and learned to cherish the work himself.

Henry worked at the mill and his bookshop tirelessly until the Spring of 1918. At that time, his daughter Betty was of age and could reliably oversee matters at the bookshop. Betty had also been, for the last several years, serving as the desk clerk at the mill. Her fine eye for detail and organization made her a natural at both endeavors. Bravely and quietly, Henry entrusted his work to Betty and, without the need for spoken agreement, Betty understood that she was to assume responsibility for the home and life Henry had created for her and her mother.

The sickness was quick yet brutal. In the autumn of that year, Henry succumbed to the flu. The memorial service was held in the warehouse at the mill, the largest space at the time to accommodate so many who came to pay their respects.

It was the first of several services in that year and in the years that followed. Betty's friend Clarence from the mill even lost his mother in '22.

But we are getting adrift.

After the memorial service, the shift in responsibilities to Betty was immediate. Henry's dedication to his work brought his bookshop to life; Betty's dedication made the shop a success. In the two years since she had assumed full ownership, she had become quite a businesswoman. She often spent the days at the shop—reorganizing, refurbishing, logging new orders, and tending to customers—and the nights at the lumbermill assisting with paperwork, catching up with the laborers, and even joining them as they passed the evening hours at the shore.

These were the days that caused her mother, Bea, such concern. She had understood her late husband's wish that Betty take over the bookshop, but still found the idea of a woman taking such a masculine role to be disconcerting. Bea had been raised to be a homemaker, and excelled at cooking, sewing, and baking. Indeed, she would have considered herself the town matron. But, no—that title belonged to Mrs. Alice Mitchell Highley, the beautiful and talented mother of Betty's friend Clarence. When she first came to town and made Mrs. Highley's acquaintance, Bea visited her in an attempt to finagle a recipe or stitching pattern. However, upon reaching the Highley's large wrap-around porch— complete with a swing and rocking chairs, honeysuckle and lavender springing up in the front garden, and the warming scent of oven-fresh biscuits and strawberries in the air—Bea could not consider Mrs. Highley as anything except the matron of the town, as well as the kindest woman and truest friend.

Now, visiting the Highleys was rather a town tradition. The lumber boys (as they were fondly called) piled into the Highley kitchen, aching for lemonade and biscuits after a long day of work. During the day, Mrs. Highley sat under the cool porch to chat with the ladies. On the cold and foggy days, she brewed a strong mint and lavender tea to serve with berry scones. On the rare humid and sunny afternoon, the ladies joined her on the left side of the porch to catch the ocean breeze with a glass of iced tea and indulge in embroidery. There was always darning and embroidery to do, what with the lumber boys wearing constant holes in their clothes.

Bea took Betty with her to accustom her to the company and manner of the ladies and instill in her a sense of good breeding. This was a futile effort. Betty tired of idle female chatter and embroidery quickly, and preferred the solitude of wandering the docks with a book in hand. She also seemed to prefer the bookshop and the lumbermill over teatime. The truth is that her father had influenced her towards his ways from the moment she was born, and by the time she was seven, she was quite set in her path of becoming a resourceful working woman.

✳✳✳

So, this woman, now accustomed to working outside of the house, sat at the windowsill ready to don her rainboots and overcoat and make her way to the bookshop. Still, Betty could smell the pastries her mother now had baking in the oven and expected to be called into the kitchen to help.

Betty sighed. Bea was insufferable sometimes, and she simply did not understand what was important to Betty. At any moment, Bea would bring up the idea of Betty marrying or helping with the housework. Betty would then remind her of the work that needed to be done at the shop and the mill so that they could continue maintaining their home…and the same conversation went around and around. It was at this point that Bea would either let Betty go about her business, or would start in about the impropriety of a woman working at a mill. When both were frustrated, Bea would call Betty by her full name: Bettunia.

This always served to end the conversation in a dramatic way. Bettunia was Betty's given name, and how she loathed it! She was called "Bettunia" for only a brief part of her childhood when the teachers called roll on the first days of primary school.

The short of it is that her father came down to the school, had a talking-to with the schoolmaster, and from then on, everyone called her "Betty." Henry assured her that the name "Bettunia" would be her secret and that she need not tell anyone. It was her secret then, and no one seemed to know any different—no one, except her mother, of course.

To Bea, the name Bettunia was beautiful. Betty knew better. To her, a name was just as important or even more important than one's profession, hobbies, or associates. A name determined everything in life. A good name could take you far, but a bad name could ruin you. The boy Cluster Owens from her class, for example. Whatever happened to him? With a name like that, it was no surprise that he amounted to nothing. The way Betty saw it, a name was an inherent part of one's identity and related to one's purpose and sense of self in life. "Betty", the pet name Henry had adopted for her, was fitting and suited her. "Bettunia" reminded her of crushed flowers, aprons, and an old woman sitting in a puffed-up armchair.

Betty was none of those things and, with her role as manager of the bookshop and clerk at the mill, she was determined never to be. If anything, she would go by "Mrs. Featherwin" when she aged, just as the respectable Alice Highley did. Forever would her full name be kept secret.

***

It was just after nine-o-clock and Betty felt the itch to go out, even in the heavy rainfall. In this weather, it was unlikely that she would have many customers. Still, she preferred the quiet environment of the bookshop that smelled of ink and parchment and sea salt to the homey aroma of baked goods. These days, the bookshop felt more like home than her mother's house did.

At that moment, Bea poked her head around the corner to glance at Betty, who was now putting on her boots. Bea wiped a hand across her brow and looked as if she wished to speak. Betty caught her eye and gave her a look which said, "not today." It was the purse of lips and the arch of an eyebrow, an expression Bea well-remembered on her late husband's face on occasion. With that one look, Betty was not to be bothered.

Nodding over to Bea as she slipped on her coat and shouldered her bag, Betty promised that she would be back for supper, and out she went. She decided to walk rather than take the car.

With a glance up into the greying, rain-laden clouds, her boots treaded the wet road with a satisfying splash. She could hear the sound of the ocean pounding against the cliffs and was content. Customers or not, today was a great day to spend at her bookshop, The Sapphire Key.

Chapter 2
The Bookshop

Betty fitted a small, slightly rusted key into the lock of a large mahogany door that creaked and whined as she coaxed it open. Entering her bookshop with a pleased sigh, she took a moment to dry her hands on her coat and take in her surroundings. The shop in its entirety was as eclectic and unique as the name her father had chosen for it—The Sapphire Key. Originally called "The Reader's Key", Henry Featherwin renamed it after years of folks commenting on the sapphire-blue lamps on each desk in the shop and the matching blue rug at the entry-way. Customers in town gradually began referring to Henry's shop as "Sapphire Key" themselves, and so the shop took on the name as a matter of course. Apparently, Henry had been given the lamps and rug by a foreign trader whose ship had docked in the harbor. Betty herself was sure that he had picked up the items from an antique shop in a neighboring county.

Though she had cleaned, reorganized, and redecorated the shop, the sapphire lamps stayed in place as did the rug. Instead of bare tables and bookshelves, the shop was now fully stocked. Clean, straight book shelves lined the perimeter of the shop and each was labeled with a different topic. The "Fiction" shelf housed the collection of fictional books and poems; and then there was the "Non-fiction", "History," and "Periodicals." The non-standard shelves include one on "Seafaring," "Lighthouse Keeping", and "Milling." Betty preferred the "Fiction" section but did enjoy a perusal through "Seafaring." The "History" section also intrigued her, especially the texts specific to the Indian tribes of Coos County, whose relatives still inhabited the region in large part. Many of her friends and acquaintances were of Indian heritage, and it was possible that even she had Cherokee blood—her father had hinted as much when he spoke of his Missouri upbringing and the Cherokee influence on his mother's side. Betty was not sure what "Cherokee influence" meant, but when she had mentioned it once to her friend James, whose Coos Indian mother lived in North Bend territory, he gave a knowing nod and commented that his mother too had the long, dark hair and oval eyes common to the tribe women.

She did not think much of this until she began to pay closer attention to her features in the mirror. She did have long, thick dark hair, which she tended to pile atop her head with pins and then secure under a hat, in line with the current fashion and suitable against the damp weather. Her facial features—brown eyes and medium skin tone—she seemed to have acquired from her father, as her mother commonly remarked on the likeness between them.

Whether truly descended from the Cherokee or not, she found the tribe histories fascinating and enjoyed learning of the ancestry of the lumber boys whose families had lived here far longer than her own family had.

With a small smile at these remembered conversations, and a longing to relive them at day's end when she was sure to encounter the lumber boys, she fastened the door behind her and began opening the shop for the day. It was quick work to part the curtained windows, light the lamps, and rearrange the books in the shop window to showcase several newer editions that had come in. Not expecting any customers for some time, at least not until the rain cleared a bit, Betty resumed the task she had reserved for such a day: alphabetizing the "History" section by author's last name and updating the shop catalogue accordingly. On any other day,

Betty might consider the task monotonous, but today, with the patter of rain against the windows and the dulcet sounds of Marion Harris thrumming from the phonograph, she was in good enough spirits.

***

Within minutes of turning to the correct page of the catalogue, Betty was just selecting an "A" author from the shelf when the bell at the door jangled, alerting her to a customer. The sound gave her a start, entranced as she was in her work, and she returned the book to its place.

Upon reaching the front doorway, she startled at what she saw. It was very well the largest cat she had seen in her life. Crouching at the doorway, it at first looked like a large, raggedy orange pillow, yet as it stood up when she approached, its ears pointed up and thick tufts of vermillion fur billowed out from its bulky frame. To Betty's knowledge, cats generally were of a small stature, and no more than thirteen pounds; only, the cat before her easily stood to weigh forty-five pounds. It was like no cat she had ever seen before at the docks. All of those cats were clearly strays—small, scrawny, and skittish. This cat, with its voluminous fur, bright green eyes, and apparent ease around humans, certainly was not like the dock cats.

In a moment, another figure appeared and Betty soon recognized it as her friend, Clarence Grover Highley, from the lumber mill.

"Morning, Miss Betty." He was a strapping fellow, with fair skin and light eyes, and strong of build. He wore a broad-brimmed hat which he only removed when indoors and in the company of ladies.

They had known each other a number of years, as Clarence and the Highley family had traveled to Coos County off and on from their residence in Ione, California before relocating to Oregon on a permanent basis in January. The Featherwins had always found the Highleys to be pleasant, and Henry Featherwin took an immediate liking to the family due to their mutual connection to the south. The Highleys had origins in Missouri and Oklahoma, just as Henry's family did. Betty remembered how similar their accents were when they conversed together, and the unique way they pronounced certain words like *Missouri*, as if it had an "a" at the end instead of an "i." Even now, there was a southern lilt to his voice that always reminded Betty a bit of her father.

"Good morning, Mr. Clarence. And what have we here?" Betty gestured to the bulky cat, which had wound itself around Clarence's legs and stood kneading the blue entry-way rug with big tufted paws. Clarence stomped his boots on the door mat and made his way inside with a respectful dip of the brim of his hat.

"This fellow was lost and wandering down by the docks. Saw him on my way to the mill. Thought your place would be the best for him for the time being," he explained.

Betty folded her arms, tilting her head at him and at the mass of fur as she considered. She somewhat doubted the creature had been wandering lost along the docks. It had a confident, smug air about it as it peered around the shop. Betty was not sure *how* she knew that the cat was confident, only that she *did* know. It was almost as if Clarence had read her thoughts, as he continued,

"Well, the cat just about ran over here on its own. I figure that here is where it wants to be." Clarence shrugged and shared a look with Betty. She was known for her love of animals, particularly the stray cats in town, as much as she was known for her love of history and literature. Perceptive though Clarence was, it did not take much perception at all for him and others to learn of Betty's soft spot.

Yet, Betty knew that Clarence had a soft spot as well. He often engaged in some kind of rescue or other, and when he was a child, he was known to bring stray animals home. Though no longer a child—he was 31 years old now—Clarence still tended to creatures, including the brood of chickens in his backyard responsible for supplying the corner market with eggs.

With the arch of an eyebrow, Betty challenged, "Will you not take it to Mrs. Highley's house?"

Clarence chuckled. "And have her throw a fit as she's fixing lunch for the lumber boys? No, ma'am."

Betty had never in her life seen Clarence's mother, Mrs. Highley, throw a fit, but she understood Clarence's meaning and finally relented.

"All right," she sighed. "Though what I'm to do with such a large cat, I just don't know." In spite of herself, she smiled and admired the cat who was stretching rather majestically, its fur gleaming like fire in the lamplight. "It can go in the Reading Room for a while where it can't get into too much trouble. I'll be back in a jiff. Please, sit down and have one of the sandwiches in the icebox below the counter. I brought along extra in case you and the lumber boys all came back before lunch."

Gesturing to indicate the location of the icebox, she then turned towards the cat. She did not so much as lean down to shoo the creature in the right direction before the cat trotted past her and straight towards the back of the shop, to the area she called the Reading Room. Eyes widening in surprise, she followed. It seemed to know exactly where to go, for it sat in front of the Reading Room door and then turned its green gaze to her expectantly. The door led into a storage room she had converted, with the help of the local carpenters, as one of the renovations she decided to take on once the shop passed ownership to her a couple of years back. She had the idea when walking around the shop's perimeter one sunny day (a rarity in Marshfield) and noticing a large window at the back with a direct view of the harbor. On a day like that, the sun would stream through and warm the room, which would be lovely for customers who desired to stay and peruse the books they purchased, she thought. And so, the storage room was transformed into a cozy haven for readers. She ordered in a pair of armchairs and a couch, and small end tables for readers to place their cups of tea upon. In the corner, she placed a glass cabinet to showcase the shop's trinkets and antiques. An old-fashioned tea set arranged prettily in the cabinet was among her favorite items.

While not ideal, it was the best place she could think of to house a stray temporarily. She turned the doorknob to allow the cat entrance. It immediately hopped up onto an armchair, the only armchair in the room with a folded blanket over the seat. Betty raised her eyebrows and murmured, "Smart cat." She was left again wondering if this cat was truly a stray, and thought perhaps she would enlist the assistance of Clarence and others to put up "Lost Cat" fliers so that it could be returned to its owner. She planned to broach the idea to Clarence before he left for the mill. With another glance at the cat, who had stared at her all the while, she took a water canteen out of her shoulder bag, unscrewed the top, and poured some water into the cap. She placed it on the floor. She then waited a moment as the cat leapt down to approach the water. It looked at her again in a way that made Betty think it would appreciate some privacy. She shook her head, bid the cat farewell, and pressed the door closed behind her. *There is something in the way of cats*, she remembered her father saying to her once. Whatever it was, the people of Coos County had their superstitions. Even Clarence, who was tight-lipped about these sorts of things, would admit that the shoreline of Coos held a certain mysticism that was difficult to explain but could be felt.

The jarring crackle of the record in the phonograph interrupted her thoughts. With a sigh, she turned to attend to the noise, though found that Clarence had beaten her to it. She watched as he deftly replaced the needle and the tune resumed.

She approached him with a thankful smile. He returned the smile and took a handkerchief from his shirt pocket to clean his hands. "Fine record you have there. Mrs. Highley has been a bit keen on this new "radio", but I say you can't beat a good record."

"I agree," she responded, and the two returned to the counter at the shop's front. It was clear that Clarence had obliged in Betty's request that he take a sandwich. A half-eaten one lay atop a piece of parchment paper. "I'll have you finish that before you go," Betty said with a smile. "And thanks for the cat. Though I'd be surprised if he doesn't belong to someone. What do you think of putting up fliers in town?"

Clarence took the last couple of bites and stood as he readied to leave. "Sure thing, couldn't hurt. He sure seems a friendly fellow."

"Friendly" did not quite seem the right word to Betty to describe the cat, but she did not let on anything different. It would seem unusual, and she would not take up more of his time.

"I'll bring along a print tonight, then," she answered, indicating that she would prepare a description and sketch of the cat for the boys to copy and post.

"Good deal. After 'while," he responded as he waved her goodbye and headed back out into the wet streets to motor to the mill in North Bend. He worked as an electrician there, and it was good, steady work. He was skilled in all matters electrical and small parts, whether machinery at the lumber mill or parts of a phonograph.

✳✳✳

After spending the next couple of hours back at her task, now having reached the "D" authors, Betty felt her mind beginning to wander to the Reading Room. Glancing at her watch, she realized it was nearing the lunch hour, and felt that she should at least check on the cat before heading across the street for a quick bite. She paused for a moment, then decided to take a sandwich from her icebox for the cat. It might be hungry. The wooden floors echoed pleasantly beneath her feet as she strode to the rear of the shop, opened the door, called for the cat, and then—

When she poked her head inside, she could see no sign of the cat. For a split second, she wondered if it could be hiding behind the cabinet or underneath the couch. But, of course, as it was such a large cat, there was no possible way it could fit in any of those tight spaces. Nonetheless, she searched about the room to no avail. The cap of her water canteen was in exactly the same spot, though now empty. Nothing in the room had been disturbed. There was not even a single cat hair on the armchair.

The room went silent as the phonograph came to a scratchy stop. Looking around for an explanation, Betty came up empty. The door to the Reading Room had been closed the entire time—or had it? And the broad harbor-view window was latched closed. Unless the cat had somehow pushed the door open and scurried past her and Clarence without either noticing, there was no logical way for the cat to escape.

She slowly traced her steps back to the shop's front and

pondered. What was she to tell Clarence now? She eyed the unfinished "History" bookshelf and took down a book she had, just moments before, placed in its proper alphabetized spot. It was a book on Coos County history and mythology. That is, the history and mythology of the native Coos people. She was not sure why, but she somehow felt drawn to that title. In the recesses of her mind, she remembered tales of the Coos tribes and their belief that everything had a spirit, even the animals with their own powerful spirits and who could harness the spirits of others.

She left the book on the counter as she locked up the shop, though did not leave behind her swirling thoughts and feeling of curious unease that followed her out the door and into the damp, damp air of Coos Bay.

Chapter 3
The Lumberyard

In the summer days of Coos County, the sun set late yet the world seemed clouded in the coastal fog. The fog rolled in around dusk, billowing in white and gray plumes. When she was a child, Betty would sit at the window, waiting and watching for the moment when the dusk pink-and-orange sky would turn heavy and grey as the clouds furled in, swallowing up the sky's colors and leaving the atmosphere white and wet. The dense overlay of trees that scattered generously across the county—North Bend, Marshfield, Charleston, and their sister counties—looked and felt greener as their roots and branches drank in the water that hung in the air. Seagulls' wings sliced into the fog, as the birds paid no heed to the drop in temperature. As night fell, the clouds gathered in heavier still, and the blink of light from the lighthouse shone in the murkiness to guide passing ships on their way.

Such a night was this night, as Betty walked along the road towards the numerous buildings, machinery, and large quantity of logging and shipbuilding material that was the North Bend Mill & Lumber Company.[1] This part of town seemed never to sleep, and Betty could feel the hustle and bustle of activity as mill laborers continued to toil away all

---

[1] The North Bend Lumber & Mill Company was an actual lumberyard in North Bend, Oregon, founded in 1900 by Asa Simpson. According to the digital collections at the University of Washington, the company owned seven miles of railroad track and transported logs from Oregon to California (Source: Can't You Hear the Whistle Blowin': Logs, Lignite, and Locomotives in Coos County, Oregon, 1850-1930 by William A. Lansing).

throughout the mill. The logging and shipbuilding business was a staple for the county, and the mill employed a great number of workers to handle the daily imports and exports. Lumber and logs were the largest and most sought-after exports with the recent years' demand for ships and vessels to transport people and goods across the waterways. The newer machinery, which was kept up and running by the engineers and electricians, allowed for faster production, bringing profit to the mill and pay to the workers.

Betty paused near a load of timber, its strong and earthy scent suggesting it had been freshly cut. From her many years visiting and working at the mill, she well-recognized that this timber came from the myrtle tree. Densely populating the southern part of the state, this tree remained in high demand, perhaps more so than any other kind of wood the mill laborers sawed, sanded, and shipped by the load to different states. Used in housewares as well as in sailing vessels, its versatility made it profitable. Betty had even seen small animal carvings and napkin rings made of myrtle for sale in the local drug store. With a soft smile, her mind's eye drifted to the fireplace mantelpiece in the parlor at home, decorated with small myrtle figurines of sea lions she had gifted to her mother some years ago for her birthday. Bea Featherwin had been delighted with the gift. Unbeknownst to Bea, Betty had a bedroom drawer filled with intricate myrtle carvings of sea creatures and other animals. When she was a child, a visit to the lumbermill with her father almost always meant that it

was time for a present. When they left to return home, her arms were full with carvings her father's friends had crafted from the surplus myrtle wood at the lumberyard. Even now, she admired the different pieces, though her favorite was a carving of a forest cat which sat upon her nightstand. She remembered that, at the time, her father had been quite entertained by the animal and had called it a "wampus" cat[2]. For a fleeting moment, she wished he was here so that she could ask him what he meant; why he found the little carving so amusing.

✳✳✳

With a soft sigh, she cleared her thoughts and entered the office space within one of the warehouses, the smell of lumber filling her senses. Her father had taught her about hard work here, and she naturally fit into the role of desk clerk, a position she had held for the past five years. As she now managed The Sapphire Key full-time, her hours here at the lumber mill were much reduced. She had helped the new mill manager, Mr. Hudson, organize the product catalogue and maintain a log of work completed so that the bookkeeping process was streamlined. The only task that required regular updating was the workers' time cards, a responsibility she was in the process of turning over to the new clerk, Ms. Millie Everly. As a highly meticulous person, it was somewhat trying for Betty to train someone who was lacking in discipline and who seemed rather more interested in winning the attentions of the young, handsome men.

Thus, Betty continued to venture to her old office in the evenings, and sometimes in the early mornings before she opened The Sapphire Key, to merely check that all was in order; that all dates on the time cards were correct; and et

---

[2] The "wampus cat" is a relic of Appalachian and Cherokee folklore.

cetera. She also liked an excuse to continue coming to the mill on a regular basis. Her mother largely disapproved of Betty traveling to North Bend in the evenings, but if it was for work her mother had less to say against it. Moreover, Betty in fact was rarely alone on her visits. Her girlfriends did not mind accompanying her on an occasional evening on their way to the shore, and her male friends, including Clarence, all worked at the mill and often offered to walk or ride with her there.

She smiled as she heard laughter a short distance away. The work day was over, but many of the lumber boys worked *and* lived here at the lumbermill. There were ample living quarters on the grounds for the workers, including single dormitories and small apartments for the men with families. All workers were also supplied with food and any other essentials they may need, out of the imported goods delivered on the Company's returning ships. The original proprietor of North Bend Mill and Lumber Company, Captain Asa Mead Simpson, had indeed provided well for his employees and made sure before his death five years ago (around the same time Betty had started working here as a clerk) that they would continue to be looked after. It is said that Asa's son, Mr. Louis J. Simpson, handled all mill operations now, though he seemed to spend all of his time traveling or luxuriating in his manor estate—or at least that is what it seemed to Betty. She did not know him.

Feeling satisfied with her look over the timecards, Betty gathered her shoulder bag and umbrella and headed towards the mess hall. There, she found many of the men spending leisure time with their families, chatting and listening to music. After a cursory glance of the crowd, Betty finally spotted Clarence. Catching his eye, she watched him nod and dip his hat to the group he had been talking with, and then strode across the room towards her.

"Evening," he smiled. "Will you stay for a spell?" he asked, gesturing towards the lively crowd.

Betty glanced over, seeing Millie Everly amidst the crowd of others she knew well, and was tempted to join them, but declined. "Not tonight; mother's expecting me back. But…" She lowered her voice. "Clarence, the cat is gone."

"Oh, where'd you leave him, then? Or did you already find his owner?" he replied nonchalantly.

Betty shook her head. "No, I mean—he's *gone*. You remember I left him locked in the Reading Room? Well, just a short while after you left, I went to check on him and he was gone. Vanished."

Clarence looked at her incredulously, as if he expected her to add something to the story or further explain. "You don't suppose he just got out when you opened the door?"

She again shook her head with vehemence. "Believe me, I checked and there was no way he could have gotten out. But, somehow, I suppose he did and now there's no trace of him." She began to falter as she picked up on the fact that Clarence did not think this was strange or interesting, and instead likely thought that Betty was making a mountain out of nothing. "It's just that, we had planned to put up fliers over town, and now I suppose we don't need to." Her attempt at explaining herself was shoddy, and she could tell in his face that Clarence was still unclear why the cat's disappearance so rattled her.

Betty felt the weight of the book she had taken from her shop, the one about native Coos history and mythology, heavy inside of her shoulder bag. She had decided to take the book with her after all. She would not dare mention her superstitions to Clarence now. She could tell he was already being pulled back to the merrymaking in the mess hall.

He shrugged. "Sorry about the cat, Betty. But you know there are always strays in these parts who seem to find their way. I'm sure he's fine."

She gave a short nod though said nothing more on the subject.

"Well, now, if you're not going to stay, you should catch a ride with James and Edith. He's got the car tonight and I hear tell they're headed your way for the evening." He was referring to James Smithson and his sister, Edith, who were close in age. James worked as a millwright, and had living quarters at the mill, but spent many weekends at his mother's house in North Bend or at his cousin's in Marshfield. James was the one Betty had told, several years ago, about her suspected Cherokee Indian lineage. James and Edith had since become dear friends of hers.

She beamed, her mood lifted at the prospect of spending some time with them, and momentarily forget her unease about the cat. "Thanks, that would be great."

Clarence called the siblings over, and within a few minutes a plan was formed that Betty would accompany James and Edith back to Marshfield. They were, in fact, planning to spend the weekend at their cousin's home, about half a mile from the Featherwin house.

Betty greeted Edith with a warm hug, and before she could utter a word, Edith began chattering away of her plans for the weekend, which included shopping in town for a new dress. She was two years Betty's junior and enjoyed music and fashion. She habitually introduced Betty to the best and newest records, and in fact was the person responsible for putting the phonograph in The Sapphire Key. Betty had resisted the idea at first, as it seemed to disrupt her vision of her shop as a peaceful escape for bibliophiles. The phonograph grew on her though, and was pleasing to customers, and now she could not imagine the shop without it.

As the three started on their drive, the conversation gradually gravitated towards her shop, and James asked her about her day.

"Well, now that you ask…", Betty answered, and with a small smile, she began to describe the events that led her to the mill that evening.

They asked the next inevitable question. "Oh, so where is the cat? Did you leave him in the shop?"

Betty had omitted the part about the cat disappearing from sight, and wondered now whether to bring it up. Unlike Clarence, the siblings seemed genuinely interested and, like her father, believed that there was something different about cats; that they could communicate with other creatures and with nature in a way that no other animal could. This could not be explained, but could be felt.

Because of this, Betty felt comfortable enough telling them the rest of the story. When she explained that the cat had somehow left the confines of the Reading Room without leaving a trace behind, and how she had felt uneasy since then, the siblings exchanged a look.

James, whose bone structure and coloring bespoke of the native blood in his veins, murmured, "You know, some say that cats can go freely between worlds and planes. Where a cat goes between nine-o-clock and noon, we may never know. But we can be sure that the cat will always return." He glanced towards Betty, who sat in the backseat with Edith, and then winked. "That's all myth, of course."

"Of course," she replied with a laugh, though sensed that James believed more in the truth of what he said than he let on.

After the Smithsons dropped her at her door, waving her goodnight and promising to see her on Sunday for brunch at the Highley's, Betty spent the next hour catching up with her mother over hot tea and a strawberry pastry (both of which were delicious) and planning tomorrow's events before the brunch on Sunday.

***

It was only after Betty bid her mother goodnight and sat on her bed in her room that she took the book out of her shoulder bag. It had been weighing her down all evening, and between today's events and James' mysterious words, she was sure that there would be something within the book to help answer the questions swirling in her mind. Turning on her bedside lamp, she opened the cover to the first page.

Chapter 4
Brunch

The first sound she heard upon waking was an incessant tapping at her window. Opening her eyes wearily, she guessed it was not yet six-o-clock in the morning. She glanced over at the timepiece on her nightstand and saw that she was correct. She turned, burrowing her face into a pillow and attempting to resume sleep, though found the endeavor pointless as the tapping continued. Finally rising with a groan, she stumbled across the room to investigate the cause of the noise. It was a pair of seagulls, sitting on her window ledge and intermittently squawking and clicking their beaks against the pane. With an irritated sigh, she unlatched the window and wrenched it open, effectively scaring the birds off and letting in a cold burst of air. She shivered as the morning mist touched her face.

"Well, I'm awake now," she muttered to herself. She watched the birds fly away, their gray and white wing tips blending into the clouds until they were obscured and she could no longer make them out.

She lingered there at the window, her elbows propped against the sill and her face in her hands, and pondered the day ahead. It was Sunday, which of course signified church service followed by the Highley brunch and all of the preparations that came along with it. She did enjoy the Sunday outings, truly, as it was always pleasant to visit with her neighbors for the excellent conversation and refreshments. While other families in the county had their own get-togethers, the gathering at the Highley's was a grand affair, with much to-do about the guest list, the menu, and the dress. Day dress for the women, now especially, was delightful (even for Betty, who spent comparatively little time on such matters). There were so many styles, fabrics, and colors for day gowns, jackets, and suits, and even the hats were both attractive *and* practical. Many of the young women Betty's age had changed their hair to the drastically shorter style. Betty, who took pride in her long locks, did not intend to change her own hair, but enjoyed mimicking the look by twisting her hair under a hat and allowing a few curled strands to softly frame her face.

Now, though, as she thought about the gown and accessories ready in her closet for the day's occasion, she was rather less cheery than usual. She had not slept well the previous two nights, and having been awoken by the seagulls, she felt the ache of tiredness and the accompanying ill mood. Betty had spent much of Friday and Saturday evening poring through the Coos history and mythology book, and then thinking about the large orange cat—wondering where it had gone; wondering whether it would come back. The disappearance of the cat perturbed her. It was silly to be consumed with such a trifling matter, Betty knew, but while she tried to remove it from her mind, she found that she was unable to shake the strange feeling that had remained with her since that Friday afternoon in her shop.

The book she had taken with her, it turned out, was a disappointment. After hours spent drinking in every page of history and stumbling through excerpts of folklore, Betty had learned a great deal about the heritage of the town in which she lived, but nothing in the way of an explanation for what she had experienced in the shop. She did not know what she expected to find in the book, or even what she was looking for, but felt that perhaps the book would enlighten her and address her strange feelings. Nonetheless, the book depressed her expectations, and she felt more confused than before. She also felt that another encounter with the cat would be inevitable, though why and under what circumstances remained a mystery to her.

She could certainly speak about Coos history in an educated way, which was at least one benefit to account for the last two nights. With a dejected sigh, she walked to her nightstand where the book lay and put it back into her shoulder bag. It would resume its place on the "History" shelf on Monday.

She then heard a rustle of footsteps in the hallway, which told her that her mother, Bea, was up and readying for the day. She expected a knock on her door, and within moments, the knock came.

"Betty, dear, it's time to get up. Come join me in the kitchen!" Bea had a sing-song voice, and a lightness in her footstep that meant she was in good spirits and would expect Betty to be in good spirits too. Bea tended to rise early on Sundays, in any case, as she enjoyed the society she kept and had, in fact, been practicing recipes all week to bring to brunch. Tired as she was, for Bea's sake, Betty would not ruin the morning. With such intent, she took a moment to collect herself, adjust her attitude, and then opened the door to meet the day.

✳✳✳

"I'm glad you decided to wear the cream and navy," Bea commented to Betty as they walked from the church and towards home, where they would stop to pick up the basket of blueberry scones Bea had prepared for the Highley brunch. Bea referred to Betty's attire, which comprised of a drop-waisted day dress, navy blue in color with cream at the collar, cuffs, and hem; a navy cloche hat; cream gloves; and cream low-heeled shoes. Betty did not mind the compliment, as she quite liked the fashions herself, namely because it was different from her ordinary work wear. During her long days at the bookshop and the mill, she preferred simpler dress and often chose a sensible suit of matching skirt and jacket with her black rain boots.

Betty smiled at her mother. "It was well worth the wait for a special occasion."

Bea took her arm and returned the smile. The church service had been pleasant and uplifting, and Bea always made an effort to attend and be sociable. She called it the highlight of her week.

Betty glanced at her tenderly. After Henry had passed two years ago, both of them had been broken for a while. Though, while Betty chose to deal with grief by throwing herself into work, doing all she could to ensure her father's shop would remain successful, Bea became a recluse. For weeks, she did not leave the house. Friends and neighbors paid visits and offered condolences, asking Betty what they could do to help. They had heaps of food and supplies from the generous neighbors, which Bea did not seem to want, nor did she want any company. For the first time, Betty was at a loss and genuinely worried that Bea would not recover. Gradually, Bea found her way back into society by reacclimating to her Sunday routine. After a month's worth of church services and brunches, she began to return to herself. Now, with the passage of more time, she found purpose and joy in her days. The shadow of grief that used to haunt her had dimmed to a flicker in her eye or in the corner of her smile that Betty noticed sometimes when they would talk of Henry.

On days like this, when Bea was perfectly happy, Betty strove to make it last. Now, after the morning's baking and service, she felt grateful and realized that she had not allowed thoughts of the mysterious orange cat to intrude on her day.

She intended to keep it that way, and not waste another moment's time on it, if she could at all help it.

✻✻✻

Betty anticipated a festive brunch, and as she and Bea reached the Highley house, she was not disappointed. The spacious wrap-around porch was engardlanded with summer flowers and bright, colorful ribbons which contrasted beautifully against the gray, Oregon sky. The side doors of the house were open, and smells of food being prepared in the kitchen wafted temptingly in the air. There was a pleasant hum of chatter as the other guests arrived, all wearing their best clothes and their best manners. Everyone was agreeable. Even the mothers with small children allowed them to scamper freely around the Highley garden and chase after the dogs (Betty recognized some as the Highleys' dogs, and others as dogs from the lumbermill). In the background of the chatter, barking, and laughter, the Highleys' new phonograph emitted soft, slightly crackled jazz tunes that would surely bring everyone to their feet come the afternoon.

The gaiety continued indoors and out. Tables in the front parlor and out on the porch bore white tablecloths and neatly folded napkins. Fresh fruit was arranged generously in bowls; muffins and scones with butter and cream were upon each plate; and oven-warmed bread and stew was being served to those who milled about in the kitchen, each taking their turn to greet Mrs. Alice Highley.

She was indeed the matron of the town. Everyone respected her, and a Sunday brunch as orchestrated by Mrs. Highley was never missed. Her husband, John, was present for each Sunday brunch, but stayed largely in the background as his wife shined out front. John worked at the lumbermill, and thus spent much of his time there alongside his son, Clarence. It was clear that father and son bonded over their mutual work at the mill, and bonded while at home as well. As Betty and Bea went inside, Betty spotted Mr. John Highley and Clarence in the parlor together, looking smart in their suits and laughing with other men from the mill.

In the far corner, she also caught sight of James and Edith Smithson and their mother Ruth, drinking from teacups as they stood around the phonograph. Betty placed her hand upon Bea's arm. "There's James and Edith. Do you mind if I…?"

Bea smiled and shook her head. "Go ahead dear, I'm just going to help Alice." In a bustle of movement and color, Bea left Betty's side to stand beside the matron, who at that moment—with an apron about her waist, arms full with a large basket of biscuits, and eye on a tea kettle spluttering on the stove—looked grateful for the arrival of help.

Feeling satisfied that her mother was all right and in good company, Betty made her way towards the three, grinning broadly as Edith turned towards her. Edith took the occasion seriously, as was apparent by her dress. She wore a lavender-colored blouse and matching loose skirt, pearl necklaces and earrings, a lavender hat adorned with flowers and ribbons, and cream gloves and shoes like Betty's. She was radiant, and Betty told her so as she greeted her with an embrace.

"So are you," Edith beamed. "Don't you think so, James?"

Her brother merely smiled and dipped his head as Betty met his eye. It seemed that Edith was convinced that Betty and James were a good match, and for some time had made attempts in that direction. In this regard, Edith was just like Bea, and Betty half-expected the two to join forces in their play at matchmaker. Betty was somewhat used to this by now, and endured it patiently. She had no plans at the moment to consider such things, nor any intent to marry anytime soon. Why, even dear Clarence, who was eleven years her senior, was yet unmarried. Of course, it was a bit different for girls, but Betty felt it should not be and was quite content in her current circumstances.

Moving beyond the moment, Betty turned her attention to Mrs. Ruth Smithson, who seemed interested in, though somewhat disconcerted by, the phonograph. She was known to not approve of music and parties generally, but seemed to place a pause on her home rules once Edith turned sixteen and she could no longer effectively forbid her daughter from meeting friends at the music hall.

"Good afternoon, Mrs. Smithson. It's a pleasure to see you," Betty greeted.

Ruth smiled, and it was a smile that reached her eyes as she took Betty's hand warmly. "You too, my dear. And I am glad your mother is here with you."

Ruth had been a tremendous help in the days and weeks following Henry Featherwin's passing. While Alice Highley provided Betty and Bea with nourishment in the way of food, Ruth provided spiritual nourishment with her companionship and gifts of candles and incense to facilitate healing from grief. She had known how important The Sapphire Key was to Betty, and had prayed and given blessings for its success. She had also been one of the rare few in town who had fully supported Betty's decision to work as the shop's manager. For that, Betty felt a certain kinship to the Smithsons and a sense that they understood her more than most.

"James tells me you've had a visitor at your shop."

For a moment, Betty was not sure what Ruth was referring to, and then it all came back to the surface. She was talking about the visit from the cat, of course, which Betty had successfully refrained from thinking about until now.

"Oh, it was nothing really. Just another stray. We all see plenty of those," she responded airily, though even as she did, she felt a slight heat in her cheeks as her words belied her belief that the cat was not "just another stray."

Ruth's eyes twinkled. "Perhaps you will see the cat again."

"Perhaps," Betty murmured. "Though goodness knows I don't need to house any more strays in the shop." She directed this comment to Edith, who had, several years ago, "rescued" a scruffy puppy from the docks and begged Betty to keep him at the shop while she came up with a way to convince her mother to let her keep it. As it turned out, the puppy belonged to a young boy (a son of a lumbermill engineer) who had been crying for days over the loss. After a stern talking-to from Betty, Edith returned the dog to the boy and grudgingly promised to stop her "rescue" efforts.

Edith blushed at the remembrance, then laughed, and was about to make a remark, when the kitchen bell rung to announce that all should take a seat to enjoy brunch.

Betty, the Smithsons, and Bea found a table outside on the porch where Mr. Dow Isaac Ball and his sister, Bessie, of the Ball family, were already seated. The Ball family was a well-known and respected family from Tualatin, Oregon and Dayton, Washington. Dow was a hard-working farmer and a non-drinker who lived with his aging mother, while his sister Bessie lived nearby with her husband and young children. They had some family in Coos County, and were friends of Mrs. Highley. On this Sunday morning, Dow and Bessie decided to drive down the coast for a visit, and stop by Mrs. Highley's brunch while they remained in town. Also at the table was a young man who was unknown to Betty. James introduced the fellow as Jackson Peters, the lighthouse keeper. He was around the same age as, or perhaps a year or two younger than, Betty, with dark hair and eyes that remained cast down as though he were nervous or uncomfortable. He wore a white sailing uniform, Betty noticed, complete with cap and neck kerchief, as though he had just stepped off a vessel. As they exchanged pleasantries, Betty realized that he and her father may have crossed paths when Henry Featherwin himself worked as lighthouse keeper for the span of a few months. She knew then that a boy apprentice worked there in the lighthouse as well. Henry had never mentioned much more than that.

She inquired of the young man whether he had known her father. To her disappointment, he merely shrugged and shook his head. A moment of discomfiting silence followed, which was blessedly broken by Edith who began launching into a summary of Saturday's events, with a full account of her visit to the dress shop in North Bend where she had acquired her hat.

Jackson Peters remained quiet for much of the remainder of brunch and then, at some point, took leave to step out for a moment and then never returned. Betty found his behavior perplexing, and whispered as much to her mother, who nodded in an unconcerned sort of way and replied, "Well, we can't all be as chatty as Ms. Edith, and he's new to our society." This effectively ended any further thoughts about the lighthouse keeper and the conversation turned to other topics.

✳✳✳

The brunch began to wind down in the afternoon, after all had engaged in talking, dancing, and enjoying the sumptuous refreshments. By the time the clock struck one-o-clock, guests slowly trickled out, bidding farewell and thanking Mrs. Highley, and all departing with a parcel of pastries and a jar of jam.

At half-past one, feeling blissfully tired from dancing, Betty resumed a seat next to Bea and for a moment, they quietly relished the afternoon breeze and waved as more guests left. Betty was about to ask Bea if she too wanted to leave, when something caught her eye in the garden. It was a flash of orange. She blinked and looked again at the spot, thinking it must be one of the ribbons that flew loose from the porch rail.

It was not. As Betty looked closer, she saw it: a bottle-brush vermilion tail, large tufted paws, and emerald-green eyes peering out at her from an orange-striped face.

It was the cat. The cat who stayed and then disappeared from her bookshop. The cat who had perturbed her for days and who had lingered in her thoughts. The cat had chosen to reappear at the end of brunch.

Turning back for a moment to Bea, she saw her mother engaged in conversation with Ruth. *I'll just step away for a moment*, Betty thought, and quietly slipped away from the table, descended the steps into the garden, and found herself face-to-face with the cat.

The cat did not run or even react, but instead sauntered towards her in a leisurely way and pressed its head against her leg. *Clarence was right*, Betty thought, *it is friendly.*

She knelt down and brushed her fingers against the cat's fur. "Well, hello there, again. I've been wondering where you had gone. You are a handsome one, Mr. Cat."

The cat made a most odd purring and chirruping sound. It was funny, almost as though the cat was trying to tell her where he had been. Betty heard her mother call her, and she hurried up the steps to the porch. Right behind her at her heels was the cat.

"Well," said Bea with a smile as Betty reached her, "It

looks like you've made a friend."

"Indeed," Clarence murmured, who had approached to bid them goodbye, and glanced down with a flicker of recognition on his face as the cat munched on food crumbs from underneath the table.

Chapter 5
The Cat

Monday morning began early at The Sapphire Key. Betty was expecting a new order of magazines and wanted to be in early for it, and also wanted some quiet time to think and plan for the day. The past weekend had been enjoyable though also unusual, to say the least. As she thought this, she looked over at the cushion in the corner underneath the phonograph, where the fluffy cat had chosen to curl up and doze. Betty shook her head, running through her mind the events of the past several days, all leading up to seeing the cat in the Highley's garden.

Bea and Betty had departed a bit later in the afternoon than anticipated, with the catch up with the neighbors and Mr. and Mrs. Highley insisting that they take a basket each filled with fruit, biscuits, and sweet peach jam home with them. It was not until half-past two when they were making their way down the road back home, and the cat padded along after them the entire way. Once they arrived at their door, the cat sat expectantly there for them to let him in.

After a conversation about the cat—in which Bea finally relented to have him stay in for the night, only because the downpour of rain had started—Betty was starting to believe she would have to find a way to keep him, as he clearly had taken a liking to her. He followed her around the house and remained by her side, and, truth be told, she was starting to warm up to him as well. He was indeed quite friendly and quite beautiful too, with a long shining orange coat and green eyes. He was surprisingly well-kept for a stray cat, she thought, but no one had come to claim him, even with the inquiries she made at brunch.

And so, the cat had stayed the night in Betty's room. He remained awake through the night, and at one point he had leapt up onto her windowsill and made himself comfortable. She rose early, but of her own volition. No seagulls had come to knock at the window this morning, and of course, why would they with the cat pressed up against the pane as he was? She had almost forgotten he was there when she first awoke, though when she saw him gazing out the pane, she was surprised at how pleased she was to see him there.

She had not made up her mind about the cat, though was not quite ready to give him up. In such a state of indecision, she did not care to finish the conversation she had started with Bea the evening prior. While Bea had allowed the cat to stay for the night, she promised that they would "finish this discussion in the morning." Betty only guessed that Bea would want the cat out and gone. While Betty was an adult and capable of her own opinions, this was *Bea's* house and Bea's word ruled the day. Thus, Betty dressed and readied herself for work before even Bea was awake yet. Taking a canteen of hot tea and a biscuit with jam with her, she left the house before eight-o-clock.

Today would be busy, as she expected the new order of magazines to arrive first thing so that the delivery would not interfere with customers. Per usual, she had walked to the shop, and the cat dutifully followed close at her heels with a slight purr in his throat as he kept up to her pace and deftly stepped over rain puddles.

Now, having organized the shop for the delivery, and taking a breath to gaze out the shop window at the still-damp streets, she pondered what to do about the cat, as the day was sure to become hectic. Glancing then at the wall clock, she saw that it was a quarter till nine, so her assistant, Elizabeth Satton, was due any moment. Elizabeth was the daughter of

Elmer Satton—head of electrical at the mill and James Smithson's superior—and she was also a friend of Edith's. She was a sweet young woman with a fondness for books and literature that rivaled Betty's. She was a fine worker and keen on helping in any way she could.

She came in three days a week, and Betty had been quite grateful for help on those days. She planned soon to ask Elizabeth if she would prefer a more full-time position. Goodness knows Betty would need her full assistance today, and had complete confidence that Elizabeth would handle the order well. She had followed through on all correspondence and scheduling, lifting that responsibility from Betty's shoulders. Yes, Elizabeth had proven to be an asset to The Sapphire Key.

Betty straightened the books propped up in the shop window. She had left a space clear for the magazine order, McClure's Magazine for July, which featured a variety of fiction pieces and poetry. She had applied for the subscription about a year ago, not anticipating then that it would be popular amidst her readers. The first issue she had displayed in the shop window, March 1919, sold out in a matter of hours. Since then, she added it to her catalogue and made a point of ordering each month's issue with additional copies to accommodate her readership. The Sapphire Key quickly became known as the primary distributor of the magazine. Since today's order was an advance delivery for the month, Betty would not be surprised to see a larger turnout of folks ensuring they received their copy.

Monday mornings tended to yield a bigger crowd, in any case, with folks stopping in to not only peruse the shelves for the new additions, but also to linger and chat with Betty about the town news (in other words, to update each other as to what happened during the time between the end of the

Highley brunch and the following morning). This was a Monday "tradition" that had started with her father, Henry, who had been more of a gossip than he ever cared to admit. When Betty took charge of The Sapphire Key, folks continued on the tradition without missing a beat. This pleased Betty, as she strived to uphold any custom her father had established. After hearing a fair share of stories by now, Betty was no longer surprised when the girls told her of dancing at the music hall on Sunday night, or the lumber boys disclosed their shenanigans at the dock, fishing or sneaking onto boats or taking a swim in the cold waters. The most shocking story she had heard was of the young, rambunctious lumber boys climbing the cliffs to the Simpson estate and trying to sneak in. The dogs on the property always chased them away before they could get close to the gates.

The bell at the door suddenly broke her from her reverie, and she turned to the smiling face of her assistant, Elizabeth. The girl had her arms full of folders. As she came in, she dropped them on the counter and then lowered the hood of her rain coat.

"Good morning, Miss Betty," she called cheerfully. "I'll just hang this on the rack," she continued, indicating that she would place her coat on the coatrack in the storage room at the back of the shop. "The magazines are scheduled to be delivered at a quarter past." She glanced back at Betty as she started towards the storage room. "I'll handle it. It just needs your signature."

"Excellent," Betty replied, thinking again what a great assistant she was.

"And then I'll…Oh! Who do we have here?" Betty heard her exclaim. She knew right away that Elizabeth had seen the cat.

Elizabeth's exclamation had awoken the cat, who hopped down from the cushion, stretched, and meowed at them in greeting.

Betty struggled for an explanation. "This is..."

"Is he yours? Oh, he's sweet," Elizabeth said, now distracted by the cat who had trotted up to her and purred as she scratched behind his ears.

Betty gave a small laugh. "Well, he's not exactly mine. He's just visiting for a while. I was hoping to keep him away from the customers today."

It was clear that Elizabeth was already falling in love with the cat, as he had flopped over onto the floor and allowed her to stroke the soft fur on his belly. "I don't think he'll be any trouble at all," Elizabeth cooed. "What will you do with him after today?"

"I'm not sure yet," Betty replied, crossing her arms and looking at the creature, and realizing that even as she spoke those words, the cat was growing exceedingly comfortable in the shop and around the people in it.

***

In a short while, the bell rang with the magazine delivery, and thereafter customers trickled in, which absorbed both Betty's and Elizabeth's attention. It turned out, happily, that they need not have worried about the cat bothering customers or getting out, for he largely stayed in his place guarding the phonograph. He was quite a hit with the customers, who admired him as they came in, though they too were surprised to see such a large cat. They immediately assumed the cat was Betty's and she did not correct them.

***

As the afternoon drew to a close, Betty planned to review her log of inventory and the past week's sales. She asked Elizabeth to ready the documents for her so that she could review them herself. Just as the two sat down behind the shop counter with the records laid out before Betty, the bell rang once more. It was indeed a pleasant surprise, as she did not generally receive customers at this hour, and pleasanter still to see who was at the door.

Dow Ball, the farmer and dear friend of the Highleys, who had stopped by the brunch yesterday with his sister, Bessie, dipped his hat to Betty with a smile.

"Good evening, Ms. Featherwin," he greeted.

She stood to take his hand. "Mr. Ball, this is my pleasure. Why, I thought you and your sister left for home yesterday after the brunch?"

"Bessie took the car back last night, but I stayed over at Alice's. I just saw her mother and brother up north last week. We all are close, you see." He had a pleasant, drawling voice which Betty found comforting, and she nodded with his explanation. He was a good man and friend to so many in Oregon and Washington. Everyone in town was pleased to see him visit and saddened when he left, but with the knowledge that he would return again soon. He treated his friends like family. He was a true gentleman with a good heart who cared for his own aged mother and his friends with equal kindness.

"I am so glad you stopped by." As she responded, she saw then a male figure behind Dow. Before she could inquire, Dow stepped aside to introduce the fellow. "I am actually here to introduce this young man to you. This is Mr. Thomas Erwinshire."

The young man stepped forward with a slight bow. He was sharply dressed in a suit, lacquered black shoes, and a pocket watch tucked neatly into his front jacket pocket. He had auburn hair styled cleanly, and as he met Betty's eyes with his, she was taken slightly aback by their startling hazel color.

"Mr. Erwinshire is from Washington near Dayton himself, and part of our own circle there. He's in the publishing business, and good at what he does. Told him he had to visit the finest bookshop in Coos County."

The young man blushed slightly at this introduction, which won him a smile from Betty. "It's a pleasure to make your acquaintance, Ms. Featherwin, and I am quite glad to see the shop Mr. Ball here has been telling me about."

"It is likewise a pleasure to meet you, Mr. Erwinshire. I know you must be one of the best in the business with Mr. Ball's endorsement."

He smiled at this. "And so too has he endorsed you and your bookshop. If you're still accepting customers at this hour, would you mind if I took a browse at your collection?"

Betty was about to reply in the affirmative, when Dow interrupted to take his leave. She and Thomas bid him a safe journey (he would return home by the next train) and then Betty gave Thomas leave to peruse the shelves as she and Elizabeth conducted their review. The phonograph hummed tunes in the background and each was occupied in their respective task. It was not until the clock struck six that Betty realized they had all stayed well after closing.

Though Elizabeth offered to stay and finish her work, Betty insisted that she gather her things while she did the same. The young man, Thomas, was already at the door talking with Betty of their mutual connections—namely, the Ball and Highley families. Betty was pleased to hear that Thomas knew and traveled in the same circles, as both the Balls and Highleys were well-respected. It was very astute, also, for Dow Ball to introduce her to Thomas, as she had been in search of a good publisher and book distributor to expand the potential inventory for The Sapphire Key. Curiouser still, while Thomas had perused the bookshelves, the cat had taken an interest in him and proceeded to follow him. Betty found this quite amusing, though said nothing to alert Thomas. It was as if the cat were keeping an eye on this new person for her, and meowed every so often as if to ask a question.

As Betty locked the door of the shop, the cat resumed its place at her feet. It seemed content as it chirped and purred, and had apparently made a positive assessment of Thomas.

Elizabeth bid goodnight to Betty and Thomas, kneeling down to pat the cat with a wistful look, then started on her walk homewards.

Thomas offered to accompany Betty, as her route was on the way to the local inn where he was staying.

"This is a smart fellow you have," Thomas commented as he watched the cat trotting alongside them.

"Yes," Betty responded with a smile. "I'm still not sure if I can keep him. But I do know he'll be at the shop tomorrow." She looked over at Thomas. "Will *you* be coming by tomorrow? I'd be happy to show you more of what I have in stock."

"If it's not too much trouble—that would be great."

They reached the curve in the street that separated the Featherwin house from the inn. "Not at all. Shall we say noon tomorrow?"

"Excellent." He dipped his head in farewell. "A good night to you."

Betty watched him for a moment until he disappeared around the curve, and then with a sigh, turned towards the house with the cat keeping in step. As she reached the front door, already hearing her mother in the kitchen, she steeled herself for the discussion that they were meant to finish this morning. She looked at the large cat, who gazed back at her with his green eyes.

"So, what do you think of Mr. Thomas Erwinshire?"

The cat gave what sounded to her like a pleased, gurgling meow. Betty smiled. "Me too."

She knew then that her conversation with Bea would have to end with the cat staying.

Chapter 6
Mr. Erwinshire

The following morning's hours transpired quickly with the many tasks to accomplish at The Sapphire Key. In addition to completing the review of sales records for the shop, an additional order request for McClure's needed to be sent (the first delivery was nearly out-of-stock after being on the shelves for just a day), and the "History" section needed to be organized. It was in slight disarray, with some books in alphabetical order on the shelf, and others in a box on the floor. Betty had never completed the alphabetization since the day Clarence had come in with the cat. Try as she might to complete these tasks within the morning, it was nearly impossible for Betty once customers began dropping by. She did not have Elizabeth to assist her, so alphabetizing the "History" section would need to wait.

She had also spent part of the morning on the cat. Bea had given in to Betty's request to keep it, as long as it did not roam around the house during the day to interfere with Bea's routine or start jumping on, or scratching, the furniture. Betty did not think this cat was the type to do those sorts of things (the cat seemed more self-reliant and mature to her), and so far, the cat was quite content to accompany her to the shop. This created an extra responsibility for her, but one she was glad of. Over the past several days, she had grown used to the cat, and felt an odd sense of comfort and safety in the shop with him there. She had not really felt that since before her father had passed; to feel it again was welcome. She now hoped that the cat would make itself at home in The Sapphire Key.

To achieve this, the cat would need its own space out-of-the-way of customers. While seeing the cat on the cushion under the phonograph, or laying across an empty bookshelf, was charming, it would not do long-term. Thus, Betty made a point of stopping in the convenience store for items especially for the cat: a floor cushion, a saucer, and tuna fish packets. The store cashier may have found these purchases to be unusual for Betty, if he had not known her. However, he did know her and assumed she was picking up more odds and ends for the bookshop.

✳✳✳

With this errand, and the catch-up at the shop, the clock struck noon before Betty knew it. She made a cursory search of the shop for the cat, though before she could conclude her search the bell rang.

"Please—come in," Betty announced, and her attention was quickly consumed by Mr. Thomas Erwinshire, who stood promptly in the doorway with hat in hand.

"Good afternoon," Thomas greeted. He held what appeared to be a stack of papers under his arm, and as he entered, he placed the stack upon one of the reading tables. "Mr. Dow Ball sends his regards," he continued. "He sent a note over to the inn this morning. He was inevitably delayed in town last night though caught the first morning train. Apparently, the passenger train was stalled on account of a repair."

"Oh?" Betty replied, as she stepped out from behind the counter. "Well, I'm glad to hear that he is on his way now."

The through-passenger service line ran daily from the southern part of the state northwards, with several trains in operation at one time. The railways were the primary mode of transport for lumber and other goods, as well as passengers. It was rare that a repair on one train would stall the lines. However, Betty remembered that Mr. Ball took two trains homeward, and it was quite possible that the other trains running last night from North Bend did not reach the station in Eugene where he would need to catch the second train.

"It was kind of him to pay a visit," she continued, and then turned her attention to the stack of papers. "What have you brought with you?"

"This..," Thomas answered, tapping the stack, "...is a recently completed manuscript from a new writer out of northern Washington. My team has done a read-through and edits, and now we're at the tail-end of the publication process. I'd like you to take a look at it."

Betty approached and glanced at the cover. "On the Level by T.Y.L.", it said, and *Erwinshire Publishing* was stamped in gray ink in the top right corner. "Well, I am no editor, but I'd be happy to…"

Thomas laughed. "We're looking for distributors, and if you think it's a good fit for your shop, then…"

"Oh!" Betty exclaimed with a slight blush. "Of course. I'm happy to consider it." She reached for the manuscript, and he nodded, indicating that she could retain the copy. "You'll need to tell me all about the author, and—if this goes forward—we'll need to discuss the details—"

"Certainly."

"—but later. I prefer a blind read-through so that I go in unbiased." She smiled, and then locked the manuscript in the top drawer of her desk for safekeeping. "Now, how about some history on the shop and the kinds of titles I stock? Then, if you'd like, we can grab a bite near the pier. The Company ship should be pulling into port within the hour, so we could likely see that as well."

"Wonderful plan," he replied, and followed her as she stepped towards the "Fiction" section. "You know, for all of the travel I do for work, I never found the time to come here, to Coos County. The closest I've been is Portland, and that was years ago."

"It's about time, then," Betty answered with a smile. "As you can see," she gestured towards the books lining the Fiction shelf, "we have a pretty varied selection. There's Austen, Bronte, and Collins, and the poets…" Her hand brushed across the spines of books. "Whitman and Thoreau, to start." She paused. "These were some of my father's favorites. This is *his* shop, you know. Every inch of it bears his influence. Everything title I stock is because I know he would have approved."

Thomas looked at the fiction titles, and then carried his gaze to the other shelves; the tables with their sapphire-blue lamps; and the myrtle wood picture frames adorning the walls. The shop exuded a rich history and shone of the deep care of its proprietors.

"I can see why you love working here," he commented.

Betty smiled warmly, feeling that he did, somehow, see why, and began to tell him of the shop's history: the toil of her father to establish it; the naming and renaming; its place in Coos County. After a quick perusal of another shelf, and a conversation about which titles the shop was in need of (fiction pieces and magazines were always in demand, while manuals on lighthouse-keeping and sailing were not), the two ventured out to the pier.

The pier at Coos was bustling at this hour. Shipyard workers and locals watching the ships come in were some of the many milling about. Seagulls and pelicans chattered and circled above, periodically diving down into the waters to catch their midday meal. Though not an area strictly for fishing, fishermen habitually made camp at the docks, leaning over the handrails to cast their lines in hopes that they too would make a catch. Fishing, like lumbering, was a serious enterprise, and it was not unusual to see the fishing boats dock here as well, when the slips were clear of the merchant ships. Boaters stored their sailing vessels here also. The long pier led up to an area the locals referred to as "fisherman's dock," which was crowded with smaller fishing boats and sailboats. Some owned boats for leisure sailing, and could be found at any hour of the day strolling the dock, hoisting sail, and readying their boats for a circle around the inlet. The waters in and around the pier remained still and calm, and thus ideal for swimmers too. It was not until the boats reached further out, beyond the sandbar, that conditions could turn hazardous. Betty had heard one too many tales of sailors venturing out and being overcome by the powerful waves.

While the lighthouse keeper and the coastal authorities cautioned against sailing away from the inlet or climbing the cliffs, many people—locals and visitors alike—could not resist doing so to be up close to the waves crashing nearby against the cliffs. The view was, in truth, breathtaking here, and one could even make their way up to the lighthouse by motorcar (or by foot, if one was adventurous).

As Betty explained this to Thomas, even sharing the story of the lumber boys' adventure one night to reach the lighthouse and neighboring grounds, Thomas admired the mansion perched perfectly on the clifftop.

"Such magnificent views from that mansion, I wager. That's the Simpson house, isn't it?"

Louis J. Simpson was the founder and mayor of North Bend, with a hand in the shipbuilding and lumber business, much of which he acquired from his father, Asa. The family was prominent and prosperous, and Louis used his wealth to fashion and improve his grand estate atop the cliffs. The

project had begun in 1906, as Betty recalled, with much to-do about the plans and construction. Mr. Simpson had made a lasting imprint on North Bend by that time, helped and sustained by the work of his father. Louis preferred to make an outward show of his prosperity, while his father had kept his head to the grindstone.[3]

"Yes," Betty answered, joining in Thomas' gaze. "Mr. Simpson lives there with his wife. I've heard that the rooms boast of views of the ocean and shoreline. There is an indoor pool and full tennis court as well."

Thomas laughed, "Yes, I'd heard about the tennis court. Have you ever been inside the grounds?"

"No, I haven't, but we've received invitations to his parties over the years." She continued to gaze up at the mansion, situated at a perfect angle for unobstructed ocean views and far enough away from the cliff's edge to remain safe from the waves which crashed and pitched dangerously against the cliff face. "They are lavish affairs, as you may well imagine, and Mrs. Simpson sends out the most beautiful

---

[3] Louis J. Simpson was indeed the founder and mayor of North Bend, and lived on the cliffs of Coos County on a grand estate called Shore Acres. His father, Asa Simpson, came to Oregon in 1855 and Louis came in 1899. The grounds still exist as a state park (Source: Wagner, Judith and Richard Wagner. *L.J.: The Uncommon Life of Louis Jerome Simpson.* North Bend, Oreg.: Bygones, 2003).

cards. Mother and I had planned to attend a couple of years ago, but we never made it, and with father getting sick in '18…" She paused, drawing her eyes down. "Well, it became quite impossible."

"I'm sorry," Thomas said softly. "I can only imagine how difficult it was—the loss—and though I've experienced it too, I was too young to remember."

Betty looked back up at him quizzically.

"I lost both of my parents when I was very small; I was just a child, and was raised by my cousins in Washington," he explained. "I don't remember much of it, and I had a good life with my family, so I have no complaints. I just…" He paused and put his hands in his pockets, searching for words. "I have photographs of them, and my relatives say that they were good people, but I have no real memories, and sometimes I wonder what they were like; what they were *really* like…"

He glanced towards Betty with a hint of sadness in his eyes that she well-recognized. "I understand," she murmured. "And, I'm sorry, too."

A moment of stillness and recognition passed between them as they stood together watching the ships make port. In that moment, standing on the docks and having much to learn still of Thomas and his publishing business, Betty yet knew him more in the short time she had spent with him than most others who had spent years with him.

The chiming of the clock interrupted their thoughts. Betty looked over at the clocktower and startled. "Goodness, it's one-o-clock. I should be getting back to the shop and let you get back to your day."

Thomas nodded and the two started in the direction of which they came. After a short while, he said, "Thank you, I've quite enjoyed my time here."

Betty smiled. "You're welcome. Though you sound as if you're leaving? Not so soon, surely?"

He returned the smile. "Leaving on the train tomorrow, actually. Though I'll be back in a month to collect the manuscript. That should give you enough time to read it, yes?"

"Yes—and I'll have a great deal of notes for you by then—you can count on that," she replied. She was not sure why, but she felt a twinge of sadness knowing that he would be gone.

"I've some work to attend to in the meantime, but I look forward to any and all comments you may have, Ms. Featherwin," he responded as they drew nearer to The Sapphire Key shopfront.

She took his extended hand. "Safe journey home," she wished him. "And thank you for the manuscript."

He dipped his head, "My pleasure. I'll still be at the inn until noon tomorrow if you need to reach me. Otherwise, see you in a month."

"See you then," she smiled. He released her hand, took another glance at the shop front and the lettering on the door, then turned and began the walk westward towards the inn.

Betty stood still for a moment, feeling contemplative as she reached into her bag for the shop key. As she did so, she heard a loud meowing sound, and looked down to see the cat sitting at her feet. "Oh, there you are!" she exclaimed. "Where have you gotten to now? I thought you were inside this whole time." She unlocked the door, letting herself and the cat inside. As the cat scampered through the doorway, he let out another sound, which sounded strangely like the word, "No."

Betty looked at the cat, who had flopped down on the

blue entryway rug. She shook her head and strove to focus on attending to the afternoon customers, who were already heading towards the door. *I must have imagined it,* she thought. This was a vocal cat, but cats did not talk.

It had been an eventful several days, and Betty found that she was looking forward to a quiet evening to begin reading the manuscript Thomas Erwinshire had lent to her.

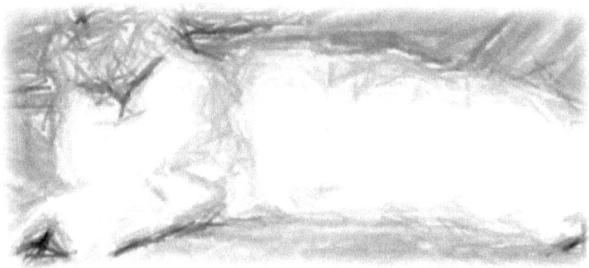

Chapter 7
The Poem

The buzz of the Highley brunch and the lingering visitors' news had dimmed by the following week, and the county had largely resumed its steady cadence. The days felt longer in the summer months and faster too, somehow, though perhaps that was because everyone stayed so busy. With children allowed to play and not cooped up all day in the schoolhouse, the pier was that much more crowded, as were the stores in town. This included The Sapphire Key, which seemed to hum with a different energy in July and August. Parents sought books to keep their children quiet and entertained, and Betty saw sales of her fiction and picture book collections soar. The women, meanwhile, continued to purchase fashion magazines, and the men to select periodicals to peruse during leisure time at the mill. The music hall downtown was as busy as ever, as reported to her by Edith Smithson. Edith had called on her several times to join her and her circle of girlfriends in the evening, though Betty always politely declined. She claimed that she had endless work to do at the bookshop, which earned her an eye-roll from Edith. This was true but, even so, Edith seemed to think Betty was just making an excuse to avoid socializing with the other girls.

Betty had not given much thought at all to summer merrymaking in the past. This year, she was too consumed with other concerns to bother. Despite the whirr of activity around her, she felt that life had become more stable within the world of The Sapphire Key—her world. Sales were steady and profits had increased with the uptick in business. Betty liked to attribute this to her customers' newfound interest in the items she stocked. However, secretly and strangely, she also thought the shop's improved success was due to the large, orange cat who had stumbled across her threshold a short time ago and now was a fixture in The Sapphire Key. Customers enjoyed coming by to visit with the friendly cat, and inevitably spent money on items they would not have otherwise. To Betty's delight, many also passed time reading and chatting together in the Reading Room, admiring the antiques in Betty's glass cabinet. More often than not, the cat followed folks in and stretched out luxuriously in front of the fireplace as he basked in the attention.

Indeed, the cat had quickly become a favorite and a beloved addition to Marshfield, Coos County. Even Bea had grown used to the idea of Betty and the cat as a pair, and accepted the fact that the cat would not be returning to the life of a stray anytime soon. She now expected the furred creature to be at Betty's feet as she walked in every evening. On the one evening the cat was not with her, she asked after him. This had caused Betty to laugh and remark, "You *do* like him!" Since then, Bea was forced to admit that she did like the creature, if only for the happiness he seemed to bring to Betty.

To Betty, the bond with the cat had happened quickly—likely from the moment she saw him in the Highleys' garden—and she could not imagine her days without him. He was well-adored by everyone, and soon was considered as much a part of The Sapphire Key as the shop's sapphire-blue lamps. As Betty went about the day organizing the bookshelves and assisting customers, a glance at the phonograph brought a smile to her face as she saw the cat curled up in his spot on the cushion (the new floor cushion she had bought for the cat went unused, and reposed in the storage room with the rest of the spare furniture).

Yes, things were stable in Coos County, and time passed rather uneventfully as July faded into August except for two developments that were relevant to Betty: the cat acquired a name, and Betty had read the manuscript Thomas Erwinshire had left for her.

✳✳✳

With the cat being a topic of interest for Betty and many others in town, we shall begin there. Betty had not made any conscious decision to call the cat by a name, nor had she spent any time thinking that he should have a name. *The animals and plants have their own spirits, their own identities, and names of their own choosing*, the native Coos legends said. Betty tended to believe this as well and, in consequence, did not worry about calling the cat anything. Furthermore, while the cat was, by all appearances, Betty's cat, she did not feel as though she owned the cat. Certainly, she did not own the cat in the same way that Clarence owned a brood of chickens or that Samuel at the lumbermill owned a hound dog. It was just not the same with this cat. The cat had chosen her company above anyone else's, and that suited her just fine.

Thus, Betty had just about put the question of the cat's name out of her mind. She began telling customers that the cat simply did not have a name whenever they asked, repeatedly, "What's the shop cat's name?" She soon realized, however, how trite her explanation sounded and she knew she would need to think of something before the customers chose a name for him themselves. Already, the name "shop cat" did not suit him at all. Every time someone called out, "Hey there, shop cat", the cat would not respond but instead looked at Betty with a glaring expression on his furred face. It was clear to Betty that he did not like it.

The day that the cat received a true name finally came

mid-week in July, when Elizabeth arrived at the shop for her shift. As happenstance would have it, that was the same day that Betty would offer Elizabeth a full-time position as shop assistant.

Betty had been pleased with Elizabeth's work and responsible nature for quite some time. On more than one occasion, she had helped with a significant order and kept track of the shop's financial records. She had even refined the cataloging system Betty's father, Henry, had implemented years ago. With her impeccable organization and strong work ethic, Betty was somewhat surprised that Elizabeth had not applied for the clerk position at the lumbermill after Millie Everly had left. Millie, who was more interested in fashion and sales, simply did not have the skills required to be an effective clerk and resigned the post just before Mr. Hudson intended to let her go. There was no love lost between Millie and the mill; within a day or two, she was working as a salesgirl at a woman's clothing and accessory store in North Bend.

The time was now ripe, Betty felt, for her to offer Elizabeth a full-time position at The Sapphire Key and thereby foreclose the possibility that she may accept the competing position at the mill.

Elizabeth had arrived on time as usual, and matched the buzz of customers filing in and out with her own energy. By half past eleven, the pace of customers had slowed, and when the lunch hour struck, the shop was left empty except for Betty, Elizabeth, and the cat. The stillness was like a sigh and a pause, until the chatter of customers would resume again in the afternoon. Betty took advantage of the moment to talk with Elizabeth.

"Elizabeth," she called from the counter, hearing the young woman gathering her coat and handbag from the storage room. "Do you have a moment before you leave?"

Elizabeth reappeared from the back of the shop, her effects over her arm. "Yes, of course," she replied with a smile. "How can I help?"

"Well, I have a question for you," Betty began. "You've done a wonderful job since you first started here. I honestly cannot thank you enough for the time you've devoted ensuring the shop is a success. I know it wouldn't run nearly half as well as it does if it weren't for you."

Elizabeth smiled and shook her head. "It's no more than you have done every day since you became the owner."

"Exactly," Betty responded and smiled broadly at Elizabeth's quizzical look. "I'd like to offer you a full-time position as executive assistant. You have more than proven your value here." She paused, attempting to gauge Elizabeth's reaction. "Would you consider accepting? If you need time to think it over, then…"

Elizabeth dropped her coat and handbag on the counter and, in an uncharacteristic gesture, pulled Betty towards her in an embrace. "Oh, of course I accept!" she exclaimed. "I love working here, and I would be thrilled to start full-time." She drew away with a contented sigh. "I am so pleased you spoke to me today. Mr. Hudson at the mill offered me a position as clerk a couple of days ago and was expecting an answer this evening."

Betty hid her reaction to this with a smile. "Here's to good timing."

"Yes," Elizabeth responded. "And what do you think? Are you happy with this too?" She directed these last questions to the cat, who had trotted into the room amidst the excitement and was now circling around Elizabeth with an audible purr.

Arching her eyebrow in amusement, Betty murmured,

"I believe he is."

Elizabeth knelt down to scratch behind his ears. "You certainly are, aren't you, Mr...."? She paused and glanced up at Betty. "Please tell me he has a name. We can't keep calling him "shop cat" forever."

Betty was about to reply in the negative but, suddenly, a name popped into her head and she knew that it would suit the cat perfectly. "Leopold."

"Leopold," Elizabeth repeated, and the cat's purrs grew that much louder.

With everyone pleased at this, Leopold the cat thus became a fixture at The Sapphire Key.

✳✳✳

As for the manuscript: it was not until the day after Thomas Erwinshire had left homeward that Betty had an opportunity to turn beyond the first page. It was a quiet evening at home, the lighting in her room just right for reading and Leopold curled comfortably at her feet, when she took the bound pages carefully out of her shoulder bag. As was her custom with any new manuscript, she first drew her fingers across the coversheet to feel the ink and texture of the paper. It was slightly course to the touch, and though the ink had dried long ago, she caught its subtle scent that lingered and embedded into the paper. It was an odd ritual, admittedly, but something her father had done ever since she could remember. She felt a whisper of anticipation as she prepared to read, straightening the stack and flipping through to check for chapter markers, when a thin card fell out from between the pages and onto her lap. It was a rectangular, ivory-colored card on which lines were printed. To Betty, they appeared to be lines of poetry. As she read them, she immediately recognized the first lines of a poem she well-remembered.

The sea-storm breeze whispers and whines
When the sky is not clear in May,
Where a kaleidoscopic pool ripples and shines
And she sits in the copse with paper in hand,
And she sits and she dreams all day.
She waits for a sign from the bird or the tree.
It is not for someone but something much greater,
With a sigh she says, "come here to me",
And she hears the breeze sing now, "be patient, dear—
later."

With a gasp, Betty let the card fall from her fingers and flutter back onto her lap. There it lay, the printed lines swimming before her eyes. She *knew* this poem. She knew every word and stanza, every image and every meaning. She knew the "she" character and how the poem was about searching for inspiration amidst a world of falsities and distractions. She knew all of this because she had read this poem countless times when she was a child in a magazine she had since lost, and had, for many years, been searching for another printed copy. This was not just a poem; it was her favorite poem. It had been part of a collection of poetry written by May Bell Sebastian. It was Mrs. Sebastian's only collection of printed works before her premature death in 1897—23 years ago. By pure chance, Henry Featherwin had kept the magazine which had this poem in it. The moment Betty had first read it, she was enchanted, and it was not lost on her that the "May" in the poem referred to both the month and the author of the poem. In many ways, the poem resonated with Betty, and she had been seeking fruitlessly for Mrs. Sebastian's full collection to display in the glass cabinet in The Sapphire Key. The collection was so rare and so precious, Betty wished only to honor it, not sell it, should she ever find it.

Now, this fragment of the poem lay in her hands and she could scarcely believe it. She may have sat there in her room for seconds or hours—she was not sure—but finally her amazement abated so that she could return her thoughts to the manuscript. Of course, the poem must be attached to the manuscript in some way, she resolved, and if so, then she was bound to enjoy it that much more. She began reading through the foreword and the summary page, which offered a synopsis of the text. Try as she might to connect the poem to the synopsis, she simply could not. Based upon the synopsis, the manuscript charted the sport of baseball in the 1890s with a fictionalized account of players of the National League and their loves, trials, and tribulations on their way to stardom. Betty wracked her brain for a long while, sitting in her rocking chair with only the sound of Leopold's soft purr in the background as evening turned into night.

There was no logical connection she could fathom between the manuscript and the Sebastian poem. It baffled her to no end. The synopsis, in and of itself, sounded interesting enough, and likely would appease a large portion of The Sapphire Key's readership. But, as the hours of the night wore on, Betty found herself transfixed on the poem, and she lay in bed staring at the card until she drifted off into a restless sleep.

❋❋❋

The morning arrived too quickly, and with it, the sound of rain and thunder. The summer storms were not quite over yet. Betty felt drowsy and achy from sitting in her chair too long, and then catching only a few hours of sleep. Leopold had left through the window at some point during the night, but was there in her room when she awoke, meowing cheerfully as if telling her all about his outing. She was not quite in the mood for conversation, but his chattering livened her out of her drowsiness and she set about to dress and make herself presentable.

With a sigh, she replaced the manuscript to her shoulder bag. She resolved to begin reading it, and with the same resolve, to put the Sebastian poem out of her mind. Still, she did not want to lose the card, and so she carefully tucked it into an envelope on which she wrote, *M.B. Sebastian*, and secured it in her nightstand drawer. She wondered if Thomas knew about it. Perhaps not, as it had been secreted amidst the manuscript pages. Still, Betty yearned to ask him about it, and to share her relationship to the poem and her thoughts. She felt like bursting with the desire to share it with *someone*, and Thomas seemed the only suitable person at the moment.

Betty fastened her coat and opened her umbrella, preparing to step out into the rain. It was still thundering, and she wondered how she could avoid the large puddles, and more importantly, how Leopold was to avoid them. Looking about at the downpour, she turned her thoughts again towards Thomas. He was back in Washington by now, and it would be silly to disturb him with this. In any case, he expected her notes on the manuscript when he returned in a few weeks' time. She would wait. She would *have* to wait, and therefore keep her thoughts about the Sebastian poem to herself.

As she stepped forward to the street, a car drove up. The driver cranked down the window a smidgeon and called her name. She frowned, wondering who it could be, though as the vehicle approached, she recognized the driver.

"Clarence!"

"Hop in," he insisted. "I won't have you making yourself ill in this weather." He leaned over to open the door.

Betty stepped into the car gratefully, closely followed by

Leopold, who leaped onto the floor of the front seat.

"Well, hello there," Clarence greeted, checking the road before him to make sure all was clear before he moved the car forward.

"Oh yes, this is Leopold," Betty explained.

"So, I see that you've kept the cat," Clarence responded with a slight grin, as if he knew all along that she would.

Betty gave a soft laugh. "It's more that he's kept *me*. He's quite the favorite at the shop now." She turned to look at Clarence inquisitively. "And I've not seen you in quite some time. Is everything all right?"

"Oh—yes," he replied. "I've been working with father at the mill, or else at home. Mother's had a touch of flu or something," he continued, and wrinkled his brow. "Nothing serious, but we're keeping an eye on her."

Betty nodded quietly. "If mother and I can do anything, just say the word."

"That's kind of you," he replied. "Now, tell me of what's new aside from your feline friend."

For the remainder of the short ride, Betty shared the few updates she had, including the recent promotion of Elizabeth. When Clarence stopped in front of The Sapphire Key to let her off, she felt, as she waved him goodbye, that she may not see him for a while again. He had always been devoted to his family, and if they needed him, then that is where he would be.

The shop felt wonderfully warm and dry after being out in the rain. As she secured the door behind her and started toward the storage room to hang up her coat, Leopold immediately went to his cushion. Before he sat down, he looked up at her and made an inquisitive meowing sound. It was if he was asking her if she was all right.

Absently, she muttered, "Yes, thank you. It's just a rainy

start to another day."

Seeming content with her answer, Leopold blinked, and then turned himself around until he was comfortable on the cushion.

"No customers for a while, I think," she continued aloud. "Which means I might be able to get a start on this manuscript."

As the rain drummed against the windows outside, she sat behind the counter to wait for Elizabeth, and wait for the chance to open the manuscript.

Chapter 8
All Night

The day passed by in a rainy haze, and it was not until the last customer left the shop with an armful of books that Betty had a chance to take the manuscript out of her bag. She had given leave to Elizabeth to end her shift an hour early. Nothing urgent needed tending to at the shop, and Betty preferred that Elizabeth leave while the rain was still light. Now, having closed up for the night, only Betty and Leopold remained in the cozy shelter of The Sapphire Key.

Betty had gathered her keys and other effects, intending to leave and head towards home, and called for Leopold. When the cat did not answer or come to her, she walked around the shop and finally found him in the Reading Room. He was curled up on the rug in front of the fireplace, and looked reluctant to move. After waiting by the door and attempting to coax him to stir (she certainly could not, and would not, pick him up), she relented and sat down in the armchair, dropping her things down beside her.

The Reading Room was very comfortable, and she had made it that way on purpose. When she was a young girl and visited the shop when her father owned it, she had always envisioned a decadent, inviting room where people could escape and dive into the world of books. Now, years later with the remodel, this was the room. It had been Betty's vision turned a reality. Strangely enough, Betty had scarcely spent any time in here, as she was often preoccupied with tending to other areas of the shop. She was also often too busy to read, which was shameful to admit given her profession.

She stood and turned on the lamps in the room, which

emitted a soft golden glow. There were no customers now; the room was calm, safe, and warm; and Leopold was snug and comfortable. She sunk back into the softness of the armchair. Now was the perfect time to read, if ever there was a perfect time.

So, with the rain continuing to tap against the windows, Betty began to read the manuscript within the enclosed universe of the Reading Room.

***

Betty awoke early the next morning, before sunrise, and took in her surroundings. With a start, she realized that she was not in her bedroom at home. Blinking to adjust to the dimness of the room, she noticed a chink of light filtering through the drapes which covered a large window; the brick fireplace; and the glass cabinet. She also felt as though she was weighted down by something. As she glanced down, she found herself tucked in an armchair, her lap covered in a mass of orange fuzz.

"Oh, Leopold," she moaned, to which he yawned and blinked his eyes at her. Then, as if sensing that she wanted to get up, leapt off her lap and stretched out leisurely across the floor.

"I can't believe we stayed here all night, and worse, that I fell asleep." Standing up gingerly from her cramped position, she saw her shoulder bag, keys, and coat in exactly the place she had dropped them. She also saw the manuscript on the nearby coffee table. Apparently, she had been enough awake to put it there, but in between finishing a chapter in the manuscript and returning to the armchair, she had fallen asleep. She turned with an accusatory glance at Leopold. "Why didn't you wake me?" A second later, realizing how ridiculous she sounded talking aloud, she sighed and muttered, "Never mind. I suppose I'll tidy this up and then…"

With a jolt, another realization hit her. She had never told Bea that she would be staying over at The Sapphire Key. She had never even sent over a note. Her face flushed. Despite the fact that she was quite an adult now, she still lived with her mother, and it was common courtesy to let her know if, and when, her plans changed. To inform Bea of her plans was not a rule, per se, and there had been many occasions over the years when they both had altered their plans without notice. Betty assumed, though, that once Bea realized that she had never arrived home last night, the rule would go into full effect. An uneasy feeling stirred within Betty.

Quickly, she gathered her shoulder bag, coat, and keys, and hurried towards the front door, not bothering to tidy the Reading Room. She felt that the only thing she could do was to go home, and hopefully, at this hour, Bea would still be abed and thus be none the wiser. Why, there had been several times when Bea fell asleep before Betty returned home in the evening. Betty hoped this would be the case, but was not necessarily counting on it.

Fortunately, the rain had abated, and while the air felt cold, the ground was not wet. This made her trek easier and theoretically quicker. With each step she took, however, she felt the journey was taking far too long. After the twenty minutes' walk, which seemed like hours in her hurry, she reached the door. She turned the key carefully in an effort to be quiet. Light-footed as he was, Leopold had kept up and stood a pace back from the door, allowing her to enter before he did. She had formed a plan in her mind: she would step inside as softly and soundlessly as possible, place her coat in its usual place upon the coatrack in the parlor, return to her room to change into her nightclothes, and then wait for the clock to strike half past six. Bea would be awake by then, and if not—well, so much the better. The more she thought of the situation she was in, the more juvenile Betty felt, as if she was a child who had misbehaved. It was a bit humiliating to sneak into her own house in this way. Still, she would rather engage in these machinations than face Bea.

As she crossed the threshold, the house seemed dim and still. Releasing a low exhale, she crept towards the coatrack, slipped out of her coat and reached to hang it when—

"Bettunia."

Betty froze and cringed, knowing immediately that her mother had been awake for hours and that she was angry with her. Bea only ever used Betty's full name when she was deeply upset. "Bettunia" was, of course, a secret from everyone else who knew her.

Betty turned to look at her mother, who sat on the settee in the parlor, lines of concern etched across her forehead. "Mother, I…"

"I would ask you where you've been, but I already know. You were at the bookshop, working."

Betty stayed silent, not really surprised that Bea had known where she was, but rather perplexed by Bea's weary though calm tone of voice.

"As your father used to do," Bea continued. "You are *so* like him," she sighed. While ordinarily, Betty would take this as a compliment, she understood that now, she was not meant to receive it as one.

Bea stood up and approached Betty, folding her arms. In

the pale morning light that illuminated her face, Betty could see her mother's beauty, as well as the creases at her eyes which bespoke of years of laughter, love, and sorrow.

"I know you're all grown now, and you can do as you please, but Bettunia—"

"I'm sorry. I just—"

"—that doesn't mean that I've stopped worrying about you." Bea released a deep sigh and allowed Betty to embrace her.

"I really am sorry. I hadn't planned to stay over and work, and I hate that I've caused you any worry," Betty murmured, tightening her hold and placing a soft kiss on Bea's cheek.

At this, Bea released her and replied, "For goodness' sake, my girl, at least remember to send a note next time."

Betty could tell that Bea had softened, and she smiled, nodding. She was tempted to say that there would not be a "next time," but both she and Bea knew that was not a promise Betty could keep. Henry Featherwin's blood ran in her veins, after all, and while Bea was loath to admit it, Betty was her father's daughter.

"All right, then," said Bea, giving Betty one more squeeze. "Shall we have some breakfast? Come help me fix some tea and throw something in the oven."

Betty would not dare deny Bea anything, and so dutifully followed her into the kitchen, where she spent the morning preparing scones, chatting with Bea, and leaving aside a plate of crumbs for Leopold. It was half past ten once Betty had eaten, changed, and prepared to return to The Sapphire Key. In her one act of good sense last evening, she had instructed Elizabeth to arrive early to finish updating the sales for the previous day, which meant that she would be there to open the shop and admit any customers. That was, at the least, a blessing, and Betty was reminded again of her good fortune that Elizabeth had stayed on full-time. With these thoughts to assuage her, Betty started towards the door to depart, but not before speaking to Bea. Though her mother's fair mood seemed to have returned, Betty made sure to reiterate her apology and her promise to be home on time to have dinner with her.

Betty felt lighter on the walk to the shop than she had on the walk home. She glanced over at Leopold, who was trotting along next to her, and commented to that effect. He responded with a vocal meow, full of inflections, and turned his face to look at her as he continued swiftly down the road. For a fleeting moment, Betty almost could understand what the cat was saying, and could nearly make out his commentary and the question in his voice.

Pausing for a moment, she closed her eyes. She was

either not sleeping enough and imagining that she could understand him, or she simply was going mad. As she approached the shop door, she sincerely hoped it was the former.

Opening the door, she turned her attention to Elizabeth, who (as expected), was working diligently at the counter and came forward to greet her.

In any case, thought Betty to herself, as she listened to Elizabeth's updates, *if I really can understand the cat, then it will have to be my second secret.*

Chapter 9
Zane Grey

"What do you think of Zane Grey?"

"Hmm?" Betty murmured distractedly. It had been three weeks since she had begun reading the manuscript Thomas had entrusted to her. She was now on its final chapter, and sat in The Sapphire Key with a pen in hand and notepad beside her, engrossed in her task of finishing the read. It was an unusually warm day in August, the sun clear and bright, and so most locals had decided to spend the day at the coast. As such, the buzz of The Sapphire Key from July had reached a lull. Betty used this time to catch up on long-forgotten tasks (the alphabetization of the History section, for one) and to give the manuscript a thorough reading and review. While she spent many hours in her shop, many other locals and visitors alike took sailing boats out on the water, tried their hand at fishing, and enjoyed the simple pleasure of strolling the pier and sunbathing. The young women, especially, took advantage of the balmy weather to showcase their new bathing suits and walk along the beach with their beaus. It seemed that nearly all of the women in Coos County, except for Betty, were out and about in the last of these summer days. Even Edith Smithson—who was more of a social butterfly than Betty—had spent the last few weekends at the shoreline with her new beau, Samuel, who worked at the lumbermill. Betty had seen very little of her lately.

"Zane Grey—the author?"

Betty finished the last line of the manuscript, placed her pen down in a self-satisfied way, and then looked up at the speaker. "I'm sorry, Elizabeth. I was just finishing this. You were asking me about Zane Grey?"

Elizabeth stood at the counter with a copy of McClure's August issue in her hand. She too looked as if she had been engrossed in reading. "Yes. What do you think of him?"

"As a writer or in general?"

Elizabeth raised her eyebrows. "As a writer, of course."

"Oh good," Betty replied, standing and stretching, and then walked over to the Fiction section to pull a book off of the shelf. "We do keep this in stock, and I recall that this sold a remarkable number of copies in its publication year." She referred to the book *Riders of the Purple Sage*, a highly successful novel published in 1912 by the American author Zane Grey, who had established himself as a writer of western adventure stories.[4] She handed the book to Elizabeth, who studied the cover with interest. "Why do you ask?"

Elizabeth set the book down and handed McClure's to Betty in its stead. "He's had a serial in McClure's for the past several issues. It's quite good, I think, if you want to take a look."

Betty grinned. "I suppose you mean that I *should* take a look." She glanced over page 17 in the magazine, which Elizabeth had marked. "Zane Grey's Greatest Novel" was written in large type across the top of the page, followed by "The Wanderer of the Waste Land-A Pageant of the Old Frontiers." As with all works published in McClure's, the piece was accompanied by drawings, and this page showed a sketch of a man in riding clothes, gazing backwards at what appeared to be a rocky slope and trees. Betty had not kept up with the story in previous issues, but had to admit that the presentation in the magazine was impressive, and the caption

---

[4] Pearl "Zane" Grey was a real-life author who wrote romantic novels of the American West: the western.

below the sketch would be sufficient to draw in any reader.[5]

Betty glanced back at Elizabeth thoughtfully. She had been an asset to The Sapphire Key the past couple of months, and was shaping into a businesswoman as well, which made Betty proud. Betty was eager to hear her ideas, and asked, "What do you have in mind?"

"I really think this one will be a success once it's published."

"You think it'll be published?" Some serials in McClure's did not go on to become major publications. Being allotted space in the magazine was like a trial-run: if the author's story sold a lot of copies and generated enough positive reviews, then it would likely go on to publication.

"Yes, definitely. It has that same type of mood and energy as *Purple Sage*. It mightn't be as spectacular, but it does have something to engage a lot of readers."

"Including you?" Betty teased. She knew that Elizabeth enjoyed Grey's writings, as his plots tended to involve romance amidst western adventure.

"That goes without saying," Elizabeth rejoined.

"And you think we should be on the pulse of it."

"I do."

"So do I."

"Really?" Elizabeth exclaimed with excitement in her voice.

"Certainly," Betty smiled, and thumbed through the magazine to skim the other sketches for the story. "I think your instinct is right about this one. The question is whether Grey will use the same publisher. If we can get in touch with them, establish a relationship, let them know of our interest, then we have a good chance of getting in as a distributor."

---

[5] McClure's magazine, volume 52, number 7, 1920.

Elizabeth nodded eagerly. "What do you want me to do?"

"For now, keep up with the issues in McClure's, and an eye on the reviews. You know how the process goes. Meanwhile, I'll check in with my contacts for news about possible publication. In fact…" A thought, and a very obvious one, occurred to her. "I can ask Mr. Erwinshire about it when he comes back into town next week." She had nearly forgotten that she had an excellent contact in the publishing arena whom she could call upon.

"Excellent," Elizabeth replied. She took back the magazine and placed a tab where Grey's chapter started and ended. "Yes, I remember that he has a publishing company. Have you heard from him, then?"

"Yes," Betty smiled. "It came through James Smithson at the lumbermill, actually. He put in a call just the other day to let me know he would be arriving this time next week." The Sapphire Key did not have a telephone, and Betty was in no general hurry to install one. The shop had survived for years without a phone, and had done just fine. In this respect, Betty was still a traditionalist.

Elizabeth, being Edith's friend, was (like Edith) keen on all things new, whether fashion, books, or technological devices. It had been Edith who persuaded Betty to put the phonograph in The Sapphire Key, but it had been Elizabeth who talked Betty into the newer version of the Victrola. Elizabeth was similarly keen on installing a telephone, but did not press it. She merely smiled as Betty explained how she had received Thomas' message, and commented, "What good luck."

"Yes, and good timing too. I've just finished the manuscript he asked me to review, and I have loads of comments to discuss with him. If all goes well, we could have another hit flying off of our shelves."

Betty was looking forward to discussing the manuscript with Thomas, as she had, indeed, found it interesting and felt it would be a good match for The Sapphire Key. It was witty and adventurous, with enough in it to appease a broad range of readers. The women would likely find the writing itself, with the vivid descriptions of characters and events, entertaining (Betty certainly did), and the men would appreciate the subject matter. Baseball was a popular pastime even here, and a good number of the lumber boys played the game in their leisure time and kept up with the National League players. She was glad and impressed that Thomas had considered her shop for it, and would thank him in person.

She wanted to talk with him about another matter as well, however. It was the matter of the Sebastian poem, the fragment of which still lay locked in the drawer of her nightstand. She could see the card now, thin and rectangular with the first stanza of her favorite poem written across it. The circumstance of her finding it within the manuscript pages still struck her as extraordinary. As much effort as she had put towards trying to dismiss it, she could not, and had, over the past month, unlocked the drawer and taken the card out of the envelope. She thought, in her utter astonishment upon discovering it, that she must have missed something on the card that explained what it was doing in the manuscript. She took it out, turned it over, and looked for any other marks or creases. To her disappointment, there was nothing more on the card to enlighten her. She studied the lines of the stanza again, lines she already knew by heart, but even that failed to provide her with any insight.

Having received the message from Thomas, the poem sprung anew into her mind. Between that, the manuscript, and Zane Grey, she had much to talk to him about and only wondered in what order she would begin. She was tempted, beyond everything else, to pepper him with questions about the card (Did he know what it was? How did it get stuck in the pages of the manuscript? Was there a connection between the poem and the manuscript that she had not figured out?), but knew she must focus on what was important: the prospect of The Sapphire Key being a primary distributor for the published manuscript. The poem, alas, would have to wait.

She had told Elizabeth about the manuscript in general terms, though was careful not to disclose further details. An as-yet unpublished manuscript was a precious item, and, if placed in the wrong hands, could lead to the writer's ruin. To be entrusted with it was a high compliment, and she had taken the task of reviewing it seriously on account of that.

Tucking her notepad into the top drawer of her desk along with the manuscript, she sighed and glanced at the timepiece. Three-o-clock. The afternoon lingered in its warmth, quiet, and slowness. Even Leopold had curled up in a patch of sunlight on a barren bookshelf. Normally, Betty would shoo him off and guide him back to his cushion, but she relented today upon seeing him so comfortably situated. The large, friendly, vocal cat truly had won her over, and her fondness for him was apparent to everyone. "Books and cats, books and cats," Edith had teased her. Betty did not mind, and nor did Elizabeth (she was almost, if not equally, as fond of Leopold), for The Sapphire Key now felt more complete with a cat in residence.

Betty glanced towards the phonograph and saw that Leopold had returned to his usual place on the cushion underneath. She smiled, thinking. Since the night she had stayed over in the Reading Room, she had, it seemed, developed an ability to hear and understand the cat. She knew, for instance, that when he chirped and tilted his head, he was intrigued by something, and she could recognize when he was perturbed or irritated by the change in his expression. She also knew when he was very happy, for he would roll about on the floor with eyes closed and a purr that reverberated throughout the room. Even Elizabeth and Bea could understand that. The funny thing that was not apparent to everyone else was the inflections in Leopold's voice. He had always been a particularly chatty cat, but to Betty, and only to Betty, he was vocal with (as Betty attributed) an intent to communicate with her. On the walks home, he was especially conversational and seemed to want to tell her his opinions and thoughts on whatever subject she brought up, or on the events of the day. This had never happened with any other stray cat or dog that Betty had encountered by the mill or the pier. At first, it baffled her, but now it felt quite normal and it was oddly comforting to be able to communicate with Leopold in a different way than if he were a human.

The only other similar circumstance that Betty scarcely remembered was when she was a child, just four or five years old. Every day for a month, a stray cat would come by the house at the same time. The cat was very vocal, which her father, Henry, found to be amusing. He would ask the cat, "Tell me about it" whenever it came by, and Betty recalled watching them have a sort of conversation, back-and-forth. The cat never stayed longer than an hour, and then went on its way, but like clockwork it was there the next day, and the day after that. Henry had started arranging his day so that he could be sure to be home when the cat arrived. Bea found this to be quite ridiculous ("It's just a cat, for goodness' sake!") and seemed to grudgingly accept it as one of Henry's quirks. "Here's your father come home to spend time with that cat," Bea would say to Betty as they watched him walk down the road towards the door. Instead of coming inside, he would sit on the porch and wait for the cat. Betty enjoyed watching him smile big when the cat arrived.

One day, Henry arrived home and waited on the porch as usual for the cat. He waited there one, two, three hours, but still the cat did not come. The next day and the next were the same. After five days with no sign of the cat, Bea had, as she put it, knocked some sense into him, and the cat was then forgotten.

Betty looked at the slumbering Leopold. She may not have understood it at five years old, but now she could guess at the bond between her father and the stray cat. It made her a bit sad to think of it, though not the grieving kind of sadness. It was the nostalgia kind of sadness she felt— nostalgia for the moments when her father showed unadulterated happiness. The hour he spent with the stray cat, a smile on his face, was one of those moments.

The Sapphire Key was where Henry had been happy, too. Taking a sweeping glance through the shop, Betty felt glad that she had taken the reins, and hoped that Henry would be proud of what she had made of it.

Turning back towards the shop counter, she saw Elizabeth at the typewriter, her glasses on the tip of her nose as she concentrated on her task. Betty waited until she was through with the page before speaking.

"Elizabeth, what do you say to closing up early?"

Elizabeth pulled the paper from the typewriter and then locked the carriage into place. "Done," she sighed, and, placing her eyeglasses atop her head, looked at Betty. "Are you sure?"

"Yes," Betty answered firmly. "It's beautiful out. Take

the rest of the day to enjoy the pier. And maybe take Leopold with you, if you don't mind."

Upon hearing his name, the cat bounced off of the cushion and loped towards Elizabeth. "He could use some exercise."

Elizabeth brightened at this suggestion. "Oh, I don't mind at all."

"Just watch him if he chooses to fish." On an outing to the pier a month ago, Betty had been surprised to see Leopold jump onto a docked small fishing boat, slice his paw through the water, and catch a fish. No one had seen him do this, fortunately, and Betty probably should have scolded him for it, but did not have the heart to when he looked so pleased with himself.

Elizabeth started to gather her things, and promised to watch him, and to walk him back to the Featherwin house on her own way back home. "Won't you join us, though?"

"No—I need to stop by the market and then mother will be expecting me," she replied.

"Well, if you're sure…"

"Yes, please go ahead," she urged. "And behave yourself," she added, directing the comment to Leopold. He was already pawing at the door, eager to go out.

Elizabeth smiled and put her hand on the doorknob. "We won't be more than an hour."

"Perfect."

With a final nod, Elizabeth headed out the door, Leopold close on her heels.

✳✳✳

After picking up a few items from the market for her mother, Betty headed homewards, where she was greeted by the pleasant aroma of cinnamon.

"Ah, you're finally home on time," Bea called out as

Betty took off her coat and put down her bags.

She smiled as she headed towards the kitchen. "I closed early today. Everyone's down at the pier. What's that I smell?"

Bea stood near the stove, her long hair tied back and a powder blue apron around her waist. She turned down the heat to reduce the pot on the stove to a simmer, and looked at Betty with a smile in her eyes. Betty knew that Bea appreciated the few days when The Sapphire Key closed early, as Bea had little time to spend with her during the week otherwise.

"Come sit down," she greeted, and pushed a plate with a steaming sweet potato dusted with cinnamon towards her. "If you wait just a minute, the blackberry preserves will be ready," she continued, indicating the pot.

Betty obliged, though was tempted to steal a bite of the potato. She knew that these came from their garden. Many families in Marshfield, including their own, cultivated a backyard garden. Bea Featherwin and Alice Highley took the best care of their gardens, Betty thought, as she had never seen other gardens that came anywhere close. Both her mother and Mrs. Highley took great pride in gardening, and as a result, the Featherwin and Highley families always had a wonderful crop of fruits, vegetables, and legumes. In Betty's opinion, the homegrown foods her mother prepared were incomparable, and she looked forward to these weekday dinners. It was rare that Betty made it home in time to dine with Bea, so she was especially pleased to do so on this day.

"And there we are." Bea took the pot off of the burner and used a ladle to scoop up the preserves and dole out a serving each on her and Betty's plates.

"Delicious," Betty remarked. "Can I try it now?"

Bea laughed at her enthusiasm. "Yes, go ahead, but be

careful not to burn your tongue."

"You don't have any cream, do you?"

Anticipating the question, Bea had already set aside a saucer of cream to serve with the preserves. After pouring some over the blackberries and potato, Betty took a bite and nodded, murmuring, "Now, this is perfect."

The two were quiet for some moments as they ate, and at length, Bea asked Betty where Leopold was. Betty explained about Elizabeth and the pier, to which Bea remarked on how spoiled "that stray cat" had become and expressed pleasure in finally getting to meet Betty's assistant. After a short time engaged in finishing their meal and casual conversation, Betty offered to clean up. As she did so, Bea set out the tea kettle and cups to brew tea later (as she did every evening without fail), and then walked over to the basket on the counter—the letter basket—where she kept all received mail and correspondence.

Taking an envelope from the basket, she said, "I've received an invitation from the Highleys. We've been invited to afternoon tea on Saturday. Just the ladies, of course."

"Oh?" Betty replied. She found it charming that Mrs. Highley, who lived just a few doors down from them, continued to send formal invitations by post rather than simply asking Bea to attend her events when the two women saw each other in town or on the street (which happened nearly every day). She found it just as charming to see how delighted Bea was to receive the letters and cards in the mail, as it was the proper way to do things.

Betty did not need to ask Bea if they were going. There was no question about it. The only question was the time they should arrive, and what they were to bring.

Bea handed the envelope to Betty. Printed on cream paper, the invitation requested: *attendance at two-o-clock for ladies' tea, no gifts please.*

To Bea, this, of course, meant attendance at one-o-clock and a gift basket of fruits and pastries. Bea and Betty always arrived early for Saturday tea, and Betty quite enjoyed it, as it gave her time to relax a bit in the Highleys' flower garden and assist Alice Highley in setting the table. This, Betty was more than happy to do, for John (Alice's husband) and Clarence were of little help to Alice. Bless their hearts, but they were quite useless when it came to cooking or organizing the house for a party. A ladies' tea was lovely, as it allowed time to gossip away from the men, and it would mean that Alice would have an abundance of help in cooking and otherwise arranging the tables outside for the get-together.

As Betty started to ask Bea what she planned to bring, she suddenly remembered Clarence's comment a while back about his mother having a touch of the flu. She was not sure if she should mention it, but Bea was so close to Alice and surely would know if she had gotten past it.

"You know, when I saw Clarence some time ago, he mentioned that Mrs. Highley had been under the weather." Betty glanced at Bea to gauge her reaction. "I imagine she's past it now that she's hosting the tea?"

Bea frowned slightly. "I saw her in town yesterday and she looked well. I can look in on her tomorrow."

"No, no, we shouldn't intrude."

"She's my friend, and I need to return a magazine to her that I borrowed anyhow," Bea rejoined, effectively terminating conversation on the subject.

Betty had expected this. The topic of illness was a touchy one, as it was somewhat triggering for Bea. After the suffering she bore, watching her husband succumb to the flu and being unable to help, it was no wonder. When the flu struck Coos County in 1918, it was particularly unforgiving. Though it had filtered out, and blessedly, there remained no sign of it now, the locals took extra care when a loved one became ill. Clarence had assured her that his mother's illness was not serious, and Betty believed him, but she was secretly relieved that Bea would be making the visit.

"Well, what do we bring on Saturday?" she asked, changing the subject to help shift Bea's mind to pleasanter thoughts.

✳✳✳

By the end of the evening, plans had been made for Saturday, Elizabeth dropped by with Leopold (who looked content and well-fed), and Betty was now in her room preparing to turn in for the night. Bea had been pleased to finally make Elizabeth's acquaintance, commenting afterwards to Betty how pleasant and polite she seemed and complimenting Betty on her decision to hire her.

Taking a breath, Betty sat down in her rocking chair, running through her mind the tasks that she would need to attend to the rest of the week before Saturday. As she settled into bed, she unconsciously looked over at her nightstand drawer. Unable to stop herself, she opened it and took out the envelope with *M.B. Sebastian* written on it, and carefully drew out the card inside.

> *…With a sigh she says, "come here to me",*
> *And she hears the breeze sing now, "be patient, dear—later."*

"Be patient, dear," she whispered to herself, waiting for her own inspiration to come so that she could make sense of it.

Chapter 10
The Gift Basket

The week flew by in a blink. Time seemed to be moving along at a quicker pace with the transition from summer to autumn. Winter would soon follow on its heels, bringing with it the colder weather, the high ocean currents and crashing waves, and the business of holiday preparations. For Betty, it would bring a sense of newness, change, and possibility. For others, too, the end of one year and the beginning of another would mark a change in the tides.

For now, though, the tail-end of summer kept change at bay. The residents of Marshfield and the surrounding areas appreciated the constancy of things in July, as the trickle of news and hullaballoo about women's suffrage and the impending gatherings in Portland had not yet reached them.

Tucked away in their own corner of the world, the Featherwins' thoughts on that Saturday in early August of 1920 were only of the afternoon tea at the Highleys'. Bea Featherwin had been preparing her gift of baked goods and embroidery fastidiously. She picked the last of the summer crop of strawberries and blueberries from her garden to make berry turnovers, which she baked until the outer crust turned flaky and golden, and dusted the top with powdered sugar. She placed these in a basket lined with a soft, white cloth embroidered with a flower pattern and edged with lace. Tucked into the side of the basket, she also placed a set of four matching, lace napkins. Bea was quite proud of her work, and told Betty that it was the perfect gift for Alice Highley. She often repeated the age-old adage that "it's the thought that counts", but added that effort and appearance turned a decent gift into a spectacular one. Betty could not agree more.

"Who will all be there, do you think?" Betty asked her mother as she pulled on her cream gloves, readying to depart for the Highleys. She also fetched her parasol from the front parlor. It was another balmy day, and though they had a short walk, the shade from the parasol would provide welcome relief from the sun.

"Oh, everyone we'd expect," Bea responded. "The Smithsons, the Everlys, the Waldrons, the Mabels…" She listed the families who were among their circle of friends, and who habitually attended the get-togethers.

"Yes," Betty agreed. "Oh, and the Sattons," she added, referring to her assistant, Elizabeth, and Elizabeth's mother, Margaret.

"Lovely. Well, shall we get a move on?" Bea asked, taking a last glance around the parlor to ensure they had not forgotten anything.

"Sure. I think we're ready to go."

Betty had decided to leave Leopold at the house. It was a ladies' tea, after all. She had given him a talking-to about staying in her bedroom, where he could comfortably nap, and allowed him to go into the backyard should he desire to be outside. He seemed agreeable to this, as he had listened to Betty quietly and without any audible complaint. Betty was satisfied that he would not get into trouble after she checked on him just moments before. He was comfortably curled onto her sunlit rocking chair, and Betty expected that he would nap the entire time that she and Bea were away. This suited her, as she did not need to worry about Leopold going on another excursion in town or causing a distraction during tea.

Betty had also closed The Sapphire Key for the afternoon. She and Elizabeth normally worked the entire day on Saturday. With the Highley tea being a special occasion, however, she had posted a sign on the door early on in the week to notify customers of the slight change in schedule. Elizabeth had offered to cover the afternoon, but Betty would not hear of it.

Thus, everything was set and arranged, and Bea and Betty commenced the walk towards an assuredly pleasant and unspoiled afternoon. Before they had reached the end of the street, they heard voices call from behind and turned to see Elizabeth Satton coming towards them along with a slim and striking woman Elizabeth introduced as her mother, Margaret. Like Elizabeth, Margaret had long russet hair that she kept styled in a neat bun at the nape of her neck. Her hazel eyes were kind and smiling as she greeted Bea and Betty. Her husband and Elizabeth's father, Elmer, was spending the day at work at the lumbermill, as most mill workers were bound to do, until time off later in the afternoon. Though Betty had never met Elmer Satton, she was aware of him through James Smithson; Elmer supervised James' work. Margaret, they found out as they chatted on their way to the Highleys, worked part-time as a seamstress. She enjoyed having something of her own to do, and was pleased that Elizabeth had found this also in her work at The Sapphire Key. She thanked Betty for hiring Elizabeth, and praised Bea for raising such a fine daughter, at which point Betty and Bea blushed at the compliment. This, though, had done the trick of bonding the two women who now shared common pride for the accomplishments of their grown daughters. Betty and Elizabeth shared a smile as their mothers walked ahead of them, now engaged in conversation about Bea's berry turnovers.

They were just reaching the Highley house and its wrap-around porch, which, in these summer months, was covered in an abundance of sweet honeysuckle. Colorful butterflies greeted them as they ascended the porch steps, and they noticed that the front screen door and back door were wide open, allowing the breeze from the ocean just beyond to flow through and cool the house.

Betty smiled and took Elizabeth's arm. "It appears our mothers have made friends."

"Yes," Elizabeth responded as they crossed the entryway. "I am glad of it."

Betty nodded in agreement, and setting down their bags, were pleased to hear several cheerful voices from the kitchen. "Perhaps Mrs. Highley has early guests?"

In a moment, she had her answer as a flurry of three came bustling towards the front parlor. Betty saw Bea step forward with a pleased exclamation to embrace the women. Betty recognized Mrs. Alice Highley, who looked well, but the other two—a slim and attractive woman, and a much younger girl—she did not know. Betty and Elizabeth stood a pace back to be introduced.

"Oh, it's a delight to see you," Bea was saying to the woman.

"Ms. Betty, Ms. Elizabeth," Mrs. Highley gestured to them. She smiled, and put her arm around the young woman. "This is May, my sister's girl, and her daughter, Florence. They've come all the way from Kansas to visit."

The woman, May, was tall and slim, with an aura of simple beauty about her. Her blond hair was swept up in a bun and her skin was tan from the Midwest sun. She pushed up the sleeve of her loose white dress and extended her hand to Betty, meeting Betty's eyes with her baby blue ones. "It's a pleasure to meet you."

"Likewise." Betty was vaguely aware that Alice Highley came from a large family, and knew that many of her relatives lived in the Midwest and South, so it would be a treat to have May and her daughter here, especially.

"Florence, come say hello," May beckoned the girl to her side. She looked to be around ten or eleven, with blond hair like her mother's though cropped short to her shoulders.

"Hello," the girl complied, looking at both Betty and Elizabeth. "Nice to meet you. I get to help with the cakes in the kitchen."

"And she's doing a great job. She'll have me beat as best baker if I'm not careful," Mrs. Highley jested, squeezing the girl's shoulders and earning a smile from her. She then came forward to give Betty and Elizabeth a welcoming embrace. "I'm so glad you're here, my dears."

The small party made their way to the kitchen with Florence narrating the cooking events of the day thus far, starting with morning teas; then the water cress and tomato sandwiches which were being kept cool in the icebox; the raisin bread; and the lemon lavender cakes with white icing. These cakes came from an old family recipe May had brought with her, and she had enlisted the help of Florence in picking the fresh lemons and lavender from the Highley garden. Florence had done so, and then left the actual baking of the cakes and whipping of the icing to her mother.

In the midst of the chatter and the sharing of the recipe, Bea gave Mrs. Highley the basket of turnovers. She accepted the basket with an admonishment ("I *did* say 'no gifts'!") that was only half-hearted, as she could not conceal her delight with the gift. She consequently insisted that each take a turnover to enjoy before the rest of the party arrived. This received no complaints from Florence, who was more than ready to eat and go out into the garden. Watching Florence skip out through the back door, the women then surveyed the kitchen to assess what needed to be done and how they could assist. After a quick run-through (put the cakes in the oven, set the dishes and silverware out, spoon the fruit into serving bowls), it was quickly decided that, with Bea, May, and Margaret Satton in the kitchen, Mrs. Highley would have plenty of help.

Despite placing themselves at Mrs. Highley's disposal, Betty and Elizabeth were simply not needed. Before they could protest, Mrs. Highley offered them iced black tea with lemon in tall glasses, and a turnover on one of Bea's lace napkins, and sent them out to the porch. Sighing, they made their way outside to join Florence, who was sitting at a table finishing her turnover and watching a hummingbird zoom from flower to flower.

"It's a shame Leopold didn't come with you," Elizabeth remarked. "He would have kept her company."

"Oh, you're right," she replied. "I should have thought of that."

"Well, you didn't know Florence would be here, did you?" Elizabeth pointed out with a laugh, and Betty realized that, of course, she could not have planned for this, and still on the whole felt it better that the cat had remained home.

Clearly, the cat did not feel the same way. Betty and Elizabeth sat down at Florence's table, sipping their tea and asking her about the train ride to Oregon from Kansas ("long and hot"). It was just then that they were wondering when the other guests would arrive, and sensing that Florence was growing bored and perhaps would not find adult company amusing. They did not need to wait long for guests or for Florence's boredom to abate. In a few minutes' time, Betty and Elizabeth startled as Florence suddenly leapt up from her chair to go to the garden gate. When Betty saw what had captivated the girl's attention, she was cross but not altogether surprised. Who would be at the gate if not

Leopold the cat, who seemed to always appear at just the right moment?

The large orange feline bounded gracefully from the gate and into the garden, greeting his new acquaintance with a meow and a loud purr as Florence petted him. Betty walked over, frowning slightly at Leopold (she was sure that he had noticed and understood the frown) and introduced the two. "Florence, this is Leopold. He stays with me, and works with me and Elizabeth at my bookshop in town."

Florence was amused at the idea of a cat working at a bookshop, and asked what kind of work he did (Elizabeth offered, "He greets and tends to the customers"). After that, Florence was greatly interested in playing with Leopold and watching him chase the garden butterflies. Suffice it to say that the pair enjoyed each other's company for the duration of the tea, and Florence was no longer bored.

The guests began arriving within the hour, and included everyone that Bea and Betty had expected. After trading introductions and exchanging pleasantries, the ladies all found a place on the porch and settled in to enjoy the refreshments and the company.

As was the way with these teas, the ladies took turns sharing their news and updates. Ruth Smithson shared the good fortune that her candle and tapestry shop in North Bend had experienced in the recent weeks with the summer bringing more visitors in. Ruth was skilled at making hand-crafted candles and wove beautiful patchwork tapestry. Betty herself had purchased from Ruth's shop many times over the years. Betty and Elizabeth had a chance to catch up with Edith Smithson themselves, and teased her about the time she spent with her beau, Samuel, asking when the wedding would be. Edith pretended to be embarrassed, but in truth, was quite smitten with Samuel and would not be upset at all if he were to propose before the end of summer.

Mrs. Everly and her daughter, Millie (the same Millie who used to work as clerk at the lumbermill) were pleasant enough, though Millie talked incessantly of music, parties, and fashion. To Betty's surprise, Edith and Millie had not met properly before, but this was soon rectified, and for the remainder of the tea, the two women sat together gossiping.

The Waldrons lived a bit further south from Marshfield in Charleston. Lynette and Lorraine Waldron were sisters, and both of their husbands worked at the shipyard.

Martha Mabel had been married early in the year, and her news was two-fold: she was expecting her first child, and she was planning to attend the suffrage movement luncheon in Portland. The news of the baby delighted the women, but Martha seemed much more interested in talking about the luncheon. Betty and the other ladies (who were largely unpolitical) endured Martha's update patiently. She lived in North Bend with her husband, and had relatives living farther north near Portland. She was in constant contact with her cousin, who would mail over copies of the city newspapers and the latest politics. Portland was perhaps the most political of all the surrounding cities, and Martha was sure to be on the pulse of what was happening. She was what the papers called a "suffragist"—a proponent for the national right of women to vote, and had been increasingly involved in the suffrage movement, to her husband's dismay. Even as an expectant mother, she planned to go to the suffrage luncheon once the national vote passed.

"So far, Tennessee is the last state needed for a full vote," Martha reported as she took a bite of a sandwich. "There is a lot of support though, so there's no doubt the vote will pass. It's just a question of *when*. I'll be going up to Portland to meet my cousin and celebrate—they're planning to hold the luncheon at the Benson hotel. It'll be the whole group of us women." She paused and looked around the table expectantly. "You all should join us. It would be such a show of solidarity."

The table was quiet for a moment, and then Lynette Waldron was the first to respond. "That sounds lovely, dear, but…would it really be advisable for you to go?"

This was clearly not the right thing to say to her. She frowned and tossed her napkin onto her plate haughtily. "Yes, I am going, and if you think it'll make any difference that I'm carrying—"

"Oh, of course she didn't mean that," Edith intervened. "It's just with the crowds and things. And the long travel," she said, in an attempt to smooth things over. "Will you be going by train? And what will you wear? I've seen the pictures in the papers, and the women have such beautiful hats…"

And, within a few minutes, Edith had drawn Martha into conversation and the small upset at the table was forgotten. The ladies all drew an inaudible sigh of relief and were eager to move on to other topics.

The conversation eventually turned to Betty, with the ladies seeking to hear her updates and news with The Sapphire Key. Everyone associated Betty with the bookshop, and many people had known Henry Featherwin. It was kind, Betty thought, for people to ask after the shop that had meant so much to Henry and now meant a great deal to her. Betty thus shared the news that was on the forefront of her mind lately: that she had read a new manuscript and had some interesting projects on the way for the bookshop. She also told the ladies of her new acquaintance, Mr. Thomas Erwinshire.

Just as she was explaining how they had been

introduced, and that he was a publisher from Washington, Mrs. Highley's niece, May, interrupted with, "Did you say his name is Thomas Erwinshire?"

Betty nodded and confirmed.

May creased her brow and then continued, "My mother used to know a 'Thomas E'—I think it was 'Erwinshire'—but a young boy. Of course, this was years ago, so he'd be grown by now."

"Oh—yes." Mrs. Highley joined in the conversation. "Sarah did mention a 'Thomas E' to me many years ago," she said. Sarah was her sister, and May's mother. "The only reason I remember is because there was some story about the little boy being on his own after his parents passed. Tragic story, really." She paused and glanced at Betty. "I'm sure it's not the same Thomas—how strange that would be—but anyway, he was taken in by his cousins and assumed their name: Erwinshire."

"Oh, how interesting," Betty replied, and her mind drifted to the day she went to the pier with Thomas; how he had told her that his parents passed when he was young and that he had no memories of them. She dabbed her mouth on her napkin and asked Mrs. Highley, "Did your sister know anything about the boy's parents?"

Mrs. Highley took a sip of her tea and nodded. "Sarah apparently knew the mother, though I never got her name. She only said that there was a carriage accident, the damage was severe, and the parents couldn't be saved. It was very sudden—very sad." She turned to May and asked, "Did she say anything to you about it?"

May shook her head. "No, mother never said much about it—and it was years ago. I was just a little younger than Florence is now when it happened." She paused and looked thoughtfully in the direction of the garden, where her daughter was still playing with Leopold. She then looked back at Betty and shook her head with a soft laugh. "But my, we are getting adrift. Surely, this doesn't interest anyone."

"On the contrary," Betty answered. She had dropped her fork and sat silently while May and Mrs. Highley had spoken, the wheels turning in her head. The fact that the Thomas Erwinshire she knew, and the one they were speaking about, had the same name was surely a coincidence. But she could not ignore the nagging feeling that there was something more to it. For some reason, the Sebastian poem had popped into her mind too, and she could not fathom why.

"I love hearing stories, even if there's a sadness to them. It's a hazard of my profession, I suppose," she continued, and May smiled at this. Betty then asked, "It sounds like your mother knew this boy's mother. Do you have any idea who the mother was, or what she did?"

"Goodness, you'd have to ask *her*," May responded, seeming somewhat surprised by the question, and glanced at Mrs. Highley.

"Oh, well," Mrs. Highley responded, dusting her hands on her napkin. "My sister would know much more about it than me." She looked thoughtful for a moment, and then continued, "I've got a letter somewhere from her, as she wrote to me when the carriage accident happened. It was quite upsetting to her at the time, you see. If you're interested, I can see if I can find it."

Betty was, in fact, very interested, but did not want to impose or seem overeager about it. "Oh, I wouldn't have you go to any trouble, Mrs. Highley. The history of it all is what interests me, really."

Bea, who was sitting a table over, and had overheard, said, "Alice, she's just like Henry, you'll remember. Always wanting to know other people's stories."

Betty blushed, and attempted to retract her statement, but Mrs. Highley just laughed along with Bea, and said, "You know, it's really no trouble at all. I'll see what I can find."

Just as quickly as the conversation about Thomas Erwinshire had started, it moved onto other topics. Betty sat quietly, still thinking. After a few minutes, Elizabeth (who sat at her right) tapped her on the shoulder and whispered, "What was that about?"

Betty looked at her with wide eyes. "What do you mean?"

Elizabeth raised an eyebrow. "All those questions about a mother involved in a carriage crash. And Thomas Erwinshire. What's this about?"

Betty shook her head and then motioned towards the garden. "Let's get some more air," she murmured, and started to stand up.

Rising from their chairs, Elizabeth told the party that they were going to the garden to check on Florence and the cat. Everyone seemed to accept this explanation and paid little attention to them, engaged as they were in their own separate conversations.

When they reached the edge of the garden, with Florence and Leopold in sight but not within earshot, Elizabeth turned to Betty expectantly. Betty had too much to say, but also did not know exactly *what* to say to Elizabeth. It was none of her business, really, but what if the Thomas Erwinshire she knew really was the same Thomas E. that May and Mrs. Highley were talking about? And, what if Mrs. Highley had information about his mother, and it was information that even Thomas did not have? In that moment, she felt that she suddenly knew too much information that she could not really confirm. She felt confused and astonished, and also felt, more strongly than before, that if there was a chance she could learn something that would help someone else—in this case, Thomas—then she wanted to take that chance.

"I'm just curious, that's all," she said to Elizabeth, who shrugged in a disappointed sort of way, as if she were expecting more, and then started towards Florence and Leopold.

The trouble was, Betty could not tell Elizabeth the *real* reason. To do so would be to destroy the confidence between herself and Thomas, and there were just too many pieces of the puzzle that were unclear to her. Thomas' words at the pier, and the poem she found in the manuscript, continued to pop into her mind, but they were unconnected and she could not make sense of them. There was just one person she could talk to about it. About all of it.

She had to put in a call to Thomas Erwinshire.

Chapter 11
A Telephone Call

Despite her general ambivalence about telephones, Betty was grateful for them now. She stood outside the office of Mr. Hudson, the lumbermill manager, somewhat nervously. It was Monday, she was on her break for lunch, and she decided that she would try to make it over to the mill. She had made it, and now she had only half of an hour to put in a call before she had to return to The Sapphire Key. With a sigh, she waited for Mr. Hudson to open the door.

***

The afternoon tea on Saturday had run a bit long. It was not every weekend that Mrs. Highley was able to bring all of her lady friends together, and even Bea was glad to stay a bit and chat with friends she had not seen in some time. Meanwhile, young Florence had grown smitten with Leopold, and, not having a cat of her own, asked her mother, May, when they could get one. This turned into a discussion about their horses and dogs back home in Kansas, and that there was just no need to have a cat too. In any event, Florence's father would not allow another pet. This all ended in Betty promising that Florence could come by The Sapphire Key (with May's permission, of course) to see Leopold every day until she returned home. This seemed to satisfy her temporarily. For his part, Leopold had had his fill of attention, and for the remainder of Saturday and all of Sunday, he lounged sleepily in Betty's room.

Even though Betty's mind was full of the Thomas Erwinshire conversation, and had already made a plan to call him, she could not do anything about it on Saturday. Once Bea and Betty had returned home after walking back part of the way with the Sattons, the day was still not through. There was cleaning up to do in the kitchen, and Bea was in a mood to chat and spend leisure time with Betty. She even took out the checkers board and asked Betty to play a game with her. After that, it was far too late to go out. Then, Sunday was for church service. The telephone call thus needed to wait until Monday.

Betty had wondered if it was even worth making a call. Thomas was expected in town that Friday and she could speak with him in person then, she reasoned. However, because she had been unable to stop thinking about what was said at the Highley tea, she finally resolved to place the call on the chance that it could help clear things up. There was no telephone at home or in The Sapphire Key, so Betty needed to call from someone else's line. Telephones, in fact, remained somewhat rare in Coos County. Only the very well-to-do families and business owners had one. This left Mr. Louis J. Simpson in his mansion on the cliffs, and the lumbermill. However, asking Mr. Simpson was out of the question, as she was a stranger to him. It would be very unusual for her to push in and ask to use his telephone. She much preferred to make a positive first impression on him at one of his magnificent parties. The lumbermill was a good alternative. She remembered that Thomas had called in to the lumbermill just last week, so of course there was a phone she could use there.

✳✳✳

Thus, she found herself at the mill during the lunch hour on Monday. She had told Elizabeth, who stayed behind at the bookshop with Leopold, that she was going to the mill but did not say why. Elizabeth had assumed that Betty was going to check in on the new clerk. Betty had just nodded and did not say otherwise.

It was cold now as Betty waited at the mill. The noontime fog had rolled in—a cloudy, heavy white layer—and Betty buttoned the top of her coat and folded her arms to keep warm. The door to Mr. Hudson's office opened then, interrupting the flurry of Betty's thoughts. Mr. Hudson was a gruff though kindly man, who worked very hard to oversee the lumbermill after taking over the reins not long ago. He gave Betty a quick smile.

"Ah, Ms. Featherwin, what brings you here? Come to check how things are going with our new clerk?"

Gosh, am I really that obvious? Betty thought to herself. She had worked hard and with pride when she was the clerk here, and everyone seemed to know that she was less than thrilled when Millie Everly had taken the position. So, naturally, people assumed that she would check in on the new clerk. She decided to go along with it.

"Good afternoon, Mr. Hudson. Well, yes, just to say hello, if you don't mind."

As Mr. Hudson nodded and started to walk in the direction of the clerk's office, Betty continued, "And, I wondered if I could…"

"Yes?"

"If it's not too much trouble, do you mind if I use your phone to make a private call?"

He blinked his eyes at the request, though seemed unbothered by it. "Certainly. No one's using it now."

"Thank you so much," Betty replied as Mr. Hudson gestured for her to go into his office. "It'll be quick."

"I'll leave you to it," he responded, and left to join the mill workers for lunch.

Left alone then, Betty picked up the earpiece of the candlestick phone which sat on Mr. Hudson's desk. She had only ever used a telephone once before, and at that, she had answered a call. She had never placed one before. Eyeing the phone uneasily, she thought perhaps she should have asked for help. It was too late for that now, however, and time was ticking away.

She brought the earpiece close to her ear and picked up the phone. Noticing that it did not have a dial, she knew she would need to wait for the operator to come on the line. After standing and holding the telephone for what felt like several minutes, a woman's voice came through.

"Operator. Number, please?"

Betty was startled for a moment, but then recovered and said the number to Thomas Erwinshire's office in Dayton, Washington into the mouthpiece. After several clicking noises, the operator announced, "Ringing" and "You're Through." There was a brief pause, and then another voice came through.

"Thomas Erwinshire, Erwinshire Publishing."

"Mr. Erwinshire, this is Betty. Betty Featherwin."

"Ms. Featherwin," he replied, and sounded pleased. "This is a surprise. What can I do for you?"

Though she could not see him, she imagined him sitting back in his chair and thought she heard the squeak of the chair's wheels as he did so.

"I…" she paused, suddenly feeling nervous and wondering if the operator was listening in on their call. "I was wondering what time you'll be around on Friday."

"Oh. Well, I'd say about noon. Does that suit?"

"Oh—yes. I'm looking forward it. We'll have much to discuss."

"I trust you've finished reading the manuscript, then. I look forward to talking to you about it too."

"And talking about some other things."

"I'm intrigued."

She smiled. "Good. I'll see you Friday, then."

"See you then."

With a click, she replaced the earpiece and set the phone back down onto the desk. She had not gotten into the Highley tea conversation, Thomas' parents, the poem, or any of it. On reflection, such topics would be inappropriate over the telephone and would take far too much time. Still, Betty felt that the call was worth it if only for the chance to hear his voice, which, oddly, had a calming effect on her.

Exiting the office, she set forth to make good on her promise to check in on the new clerk before she made her way back to The Sapphire Key.

✳✳✳

The remainder of the week passed rather uneventfully. Customers came and went, and Florence did stop in several times with her mother to visit with Leopold. This pleased the cat, and pleased Betty and Elizabeth as well, as it gave them a further opportunity to get to know May. Betty still had not said another word to anyone about the Highley tea "Thomas E." conversation, and May did not bring it up again. Betty kept her lingering questions regarding the Sebastian poem to herself also. She felt it best to leave it be, for now, and perhaps she would not even bother Thomas Erwinshire with it. She wondered if she was overthinking everything, and making too much out of nothing. With these thoughts in her mind, she was at the point of forgetting all about the Highley tea when she received a telegram at the bookshop from Mrs. Alice Highley. The telegram stated that she would stop in next week, and to please respond with a convenient day and time. Mrs. Highley did not indicate what her visit would be about, but Betty hoped that she was correct in her assumption. Perhaps Mrs. Highley had found the letter from her sister that explained more about the carriage accident involving two forgotten parents. This was sufficient to stir up Betty's interest again.

Thus, with Thomas' arrival in town and Mrs. Highley's visit to look forward to, Betty was eager for Friday to arrive. On Thursday evening, just before closing, she spent some time looking through her notes on the manuscript and refreshing herself on some of the questions she had prepared. She also took out the marked copy of McClure's August issue. Time permitting, she would gather Thomas' input on Zane Grey's new novel as well.

"You're looking forward to Mr. Erwinshire coming back into town."

Betty glanced up from her task and saw Elizabeth at the door, purse in hand and coat over her arm. Betty smiled. "What gave me away?"

"Apart from what you're doing now," Elizabeth replied, "You've been hinting at it all week. That must be one home run of a manuscript."

Betty laughed and dipped her head, acknowledging Elizabeth's clever pun, though wondering if there was something else behind her words too.

"Well, good night, and don't stay too late. I'll see you in the morning?"

"Yes," Betty replied, and waved her out. "Have a safe walk home."

With a backwards wave, Elizabeth left the store, the bell on the door jangling. Left in the calm quiet of the bookshop, Betty looked around for Leopold and found him reliably in his spot on the cushion. She softly beckoned him to her, and he stretched then bounced over to her, purring as she stroked his head.

"Well, Leopold, what do you think?"

He made an inquisitive chirping sound and looked at her

with his large eyes, and then placed a paw on her knee.

"Hmm," she murmured. "We do understand each other, don't we?"

He purred, then trotted to the front door and stood kneading the entryway rug.

Betty laughed. "And that's your way of telling me it's time to go. All right, all right." She began to gather her effects and turn down the lamps so that the bookshop was left in darkness. "I think we're ready." She paused and searched through her shoulder bag. "Wait, where are my keys? I must have left them…"

She felt and heard Leopold rustle around her, and in a few moments, he returned, pawing at her feet. She knelt down to see what was the matter, and saw her key ring with her collection of keys on it in Leopold's mouth. "How did you…" she started to say, but did not finish her question. Shaking her head fondly, she took the keys from him and proceeded to lock up.

The two walked together back home in the kind of companionable silence that happens between friends who know each other so well that words are unnecessary.

✳✳✳

"…and here is the non-fiction section. I think what you're looking for is there. Sailing, science of navigation, shipbuilding—our small but hearty nautical selection." On the following day, Betty was in The Sapphire Key assisting customers. She gestured towards a bookshelf, guiding a customer who had come into the bookshop looking for manuals related to seafaring. While she herself may not be well-versed in that subject, she was nothing if not an expert in her inventory. She knew every single title she stocked, and where it was located in the shop. She also had a general working knowledge of each topic and subtopic. On the subject of sailing, for example, she knew about the practice and art of knots, and was aware that she stocked a text about knot tying and could guide a customer with that specific request. The customer now in her store did not have a specific request, which was even better. Betty could show the customer the entire section to peruse, and more than likely he would come up to the counter later wanting to purchase two or three titles.

"Miss, I'm wondering if you could assist me as well."

Hearing the male voice behind her, she politely excused herself from the customer—who was now poring over a book on navigation—to assist the person who had just entered. As she turned around, she startled in a pleasant surprise. Standing in the doorway, hat in hand, and wearing a neat three-piece gray suit and a warm smile, was Thomas Erwinshire.

"Mr. Erwinshire," she exclaimed. "Why, it's not yet eleven and you're here." She was so pleased to see him that it caught her slightly off guard, and she smoothed her curled hair behind her ears to collect herself.

He walked forward and dipped his head with a slight bow. "I hope I've not thrown a wrench into your day."

"On the contrary," she replied.

"My train arrived early and I thought I'd stop here to say hello first," he explained, and then smiled. "I told you I'd be in town at about noon, and I've kept to it."

"You certainly have, and I'm glad you stopped in." She smiled again, and gestured for him to sit down at an open table. "I have some customers to attend to, but I'm eager to catch up. Are you free for lunch?"

"I'm not, actually," he replied with a slight frown. "I've a few letters to write and post. Didn't quite get to them on the train. But," he looked up at her expectantly. "How about dinner—my treat? I can pick you up at six."

"Yes, that sounds good," she answered, and then nodded to greet another customer who walked through the door.

"Good." He looked as though he wanted to say more, but stopped himself upon seeing her distracted with the customer.

"Before you leave—" Betty stepped out from behind the counter to halt his departure. "—pop into the Reading Room for a moment and say hello to Elizabeth? She'll be happy to see you, and glad to have a break."

He nodded and then turned to make his way down the hall. In the time it took for him to greet Elizabeth, pet Leopold, and then return to the front of the shop, five additional customers came in during the "pre-luncheon rush" and Betty was too occupied to tell Thomas goodbye. She was glad he had stopped by, however, and was looking forward to their impending conversation even more than before.

✳✳✳

Thomas arrived on time as the clock struck six. Betty just finished closing the shop, and Elizabeth had already left for the day. She made sure to send a note home to Bea, letting her mother know of her plans for the evening.

As Thomas walked into the shop, she noticed that he had changed into a different, though just as striking, suit. This was likely because the one she saw him in earlier in the day had been from his ride on the train. It was habit to change after travel, even if the train was pristine and the voyage refreshing.

"Good evening," he greeted.

"Good evening," she replied, then smiled as Leopold trotted past her to wind around Thomas' feet. "He remembers you."

"I remember you, too," Thomas murmured, and bent

down to pat the cat. "Hello Leopold." He meowed in greeting and then sat down by the door, indicating that he was ready to leave.

"I'm just about ready. I'll just fetch my coat and then we can be off," Betty said, taking one final look inside of her shoulder bag to make sure she had not forgotten anything. Satisfied that she had not, she looked up at Thomas and added, "Do you mind if Leopold comes with us? I don't like him wandering at night."

"Of course not," he replied. "We'll wait here for you, then all walk out together."

Betty smiled in response and turned to fetch her things from the storage room.

"And I hate to ask this...but do you have a place in mind?" he continued. "I'm sorry; I find it rather unorthodox to ask a lady to dinner without having a plan in place."

She returned from the storage room with bag, keys, and coat, and shook her head with a soft laugh at his sense of propriety. "Nonsense. You're new to the area, and I'd already thought of a place anyhow."

"I see," he responded with a smile, and then extended a hand to assist her in putting on her coat.

"We'll go to town, near the docks to a cheery little café. There's an excellent view of the water and it's not too noisy."

"Sounds good," he replied as she locked the door and they stepped out into the cool evening. The sun was still out, though the breeze was picking up and the feel of the ocean mist was in the air. "How was the rest of your afternoon?" he asked.

"Oh, busy, but not so much more than usual. Leopold had some company—a girl named Florence, who is the great niece of one of our neighbors. She and her mother came over from the Midwest to visit..." She told him a brief and condensed version of the Saturday tea, namely how Leopold had made Florence's acquaintance.

"Sounds like it was a nice treat for him, and an altogether pleasant afternoon," he commented.

"It was," she agreed, though in the back of her mind knew she had not yet told him *all* of what had occurred last Saturday. "How was the journey here? And where are you staying?"

He proceeded to recount the train ride and the reading and editing he had done to keep himself occupied and productive for the journey's duration. The through-passenger service line these days was comfortable and stately, with each carriage able to carry up to six passengers with wide-apart seating, and accommodations for long journeys and overnight stays. While there were others in Thomas' carriage, he kept largely to himself and took advantage of the time to work.

"It was quite nice to have the time to run through correspondence and work on some edits uninterrupted," he told her.

"I can imagine," she replied, only thinking of how much she could accomplish away from the constant buzz of customers and distractors at The Sapphire Key. "Do you edit manuscripts yourself, then?"

"Not strictly," he replied with a smile. "That's mostly left to my staff, but I do enjoy it. I slipped an article into my bag just for that purpose."

Along the rest of their walk, he told her more about his publishing business. It was small compared to the larger enterprises. Besides him and his associate (who spent a great deal of time traveling and was rarely at their office in Washington), they had a staff of five. This included a secretary and editors.

"Our editors are quite good and don't care for me to look over their shoulders, so I don't have much opportunity at all for editing while I'm in the office."

Betty laughed. "Well, I don't blame them. But I can see why you'd enjoy it."

They had reached their destination at this point. As Betty had described, it was a cheerful café with views of the water and docked boats. The building was angled in such a way that guests could see the sun setting like an orange glow on the skyline in the evenings. It was quite picturesque.

"You can?" he responded to her statement. "Most people think it quite odd to enjoy something as mundane as editing."

"Not more mundane than rummaging through historical documents and archives."

"Touché."

In a moment, the host greeted them and showed them to a table, welcoming them in and assuring that a waiter would come by shortly. Betty and Thomas continued on with their conversation in the meanwhile, and in what seemed like no time at all, they were brought refreshments. Even Leopold was given a saucer of water and a plate of tuna fish. After they received their orders of soup and salad, the discussion eventually turned to the manuscript Thomas had left with Betty.

"So, what did you think?" he asked her, taking a sip from his glass of iced tea. "Is it a good fit for The Sapphire Key?"

"Yes, I think it is. I found it well-written, and entertaining. I think the subject matter will appeal to a good portion of our readership."

Thomas nodded. "Good to hear. That is what I hoped for."

Betty smiled, and reached into her shoulder bag for the manuscript, along with her notebook upon which she had written comments and questions. "I've done a full review," she said, placing the texts on the table beside her plate. "And I have some questions, but nothing earth-shattering." She paused and flipped through the pages of her notepad, thinking of where she might start. As she turned another page, she saw that she had written, in the corner and in small font, "Sebastian." She felt her cheeks flush suddenly.

"Well, please, by all means, share them with me." Thomas' voice interrupted her racing thoughts. "And I recall promising to tell you about the author." He paused and looked at her over the rim of his glass. "If that goes well, we can get into the business details."

When she failed to respond right away, he continued, "Ms. Featherwin?"

Upon hearing her name, she at last looked up into his hazel eyes, which studied her with a note of inquisitiveness. Considering him then, sitting across from her in the orange glow of the café, and out of earshot of the other customers, she felt compelled to speak what was on her mind.

"I am amenable to all of that, and I want to talk to you more about the manuscript. But, first…" she paused, and flipped to the back of her notepad. There, she had re-written the lines to the Sebastian poem in a feeble attempt to make sense of the words and their possible connection to the manuscript. "…I'd like to talk about what was inside." She had had a bee in her bonnet about the poem, and goodness knows she had been bursting to finally talk about it.

Thomas looked rightfully puzzled, and remarked, "You strike me as a woman of great intellect, and I feel as though I've met my match there. But I confess that what you've just said went over my head a bit."

Betty turned the notepad so that it faced him, showing him the page with the lines of the poem. She was not sure whether it would mean anything to him, but wanted him to see the poem before she offered an explanation. He took a moment to skim through. He drew in a breath, and it was then that she knew. He recognized the poem.

Thomas continued looking down at the page for a few moments, frowning. Betty remained still and quiet until he looked at her again. His tone was soft, though curious. "I know this poem. Why do you have it written here? And what does it have to do with the manuscript?"

Betty swallowed. "I was hoping you would recognize it. When I first opened the manuscript, a card fell out from between the pages. On that card was written the first stanza of that poem." She paused for him to respond, and what he next said surprised her.

"Oh gosh," he murmured with a sigh. "It sounds like you found my bookmark."

Betty's eyes widened. No, she was not expecting that. "What?"

Thomas smiled at her expression. "I've been using this card as a bookmark for years, and I'd recently lost it and wondered where I left it. Apparently, I stuck it inside the manuscript when I was reading it, and forgot to take the card out before I gave it to you."

"But…" Betty was lost for words for a moment at the utter simplicity of Thomas' explanation, as compared to her much more complicated thoughts about it. "But…what about the poem?"

"Oh, well, that's a bit of a story. You remember that I told you about my parents? That I have no real memories of them?"

She nodded silently.

"Well," he continued, and turned the notepad so that it again faced her. "That poem is one of the few mementos I *do* have."

Betty was on tenterhooks, and Thomas must have seen the question in her eyes, for he continued, "I'm told that my mother wrote those lines not long before she passed."

In that moment, it felt that the world had shifted and realigned to make sense of things that did not make sense before. At the same time, Betty's eyes watered and a million thoughts and questions sprung in her mind. All she could think to say was, "Do you know, that's my favorite poem?"

Chapter 12
Realization

Betty had explained to Thomas that she read his mother's poem in a magazine many years ago, and that the words had just stayed with her. She could scarcely believe that she would encounter the poem again, and admitted to Thomas that she was quite shocked when she found his bookmark with the words of the poem written on it. More astonishing still was the idea that she met, and was sitting with, the poet's son.

Thomas equally found the coincidence to be amazing. He told her that the poem had lingered with him all of these years as well, because he felt that it carried a piece of his mother. Every time he read the words, he felt that he was getting a glimpse of the woman he had yearned to know. He then admitted that, although his cousins had raised him and were like parents to him, there had always been a part of him that wanted to know more of his mother and father.

Upon hearing Thomas disclose this, and seeing the shadow of sadness across his face, Betty felt that now was the time to tell him about last Saturday's tea.

"You know…," she began softly. "…that all of us ladies had tea last Saturday."

He nodded, though looked slightly puzzled at what he imagined to be a sudden change of subject.

"Well, your name came up, actually. I had mentioned that we met, and that you came by The Sapphire Key. And then, Mrs. Alice Highley, who you may know—"

"Yes, I know her" he interrupted, then paused to correct himself. "Well, only second-hand, through Mr. Dow Ball."

Betty nodded, then continued, "Mrs. Highley and her

niece and I fell into a conversation." She shook her head then, finding the right words to explain it. "They think they know, or used to know, someone with the same name as yours, and that person's family. It was quite odd."

Thomas knit his eyebrows in perplexity. "What exactly did they say?"

Betty began to recount the details of the conversation while Thomas listened patiently. As she finished, ending on the supposed carriage accident responsible for the death of "Thomas E.'s" parents, she added, "It's probably someone unconnected to you. At least…" she paused and glanced down at Leopold, who had been sitting still by her feet while she recounted the story. His green gaze gave her faith. "At least that's what Mrs. Highley was inclined to think," she finished, and returned her eyes to Thomas'.

His expression shifted slightly, as if he were comprehending and reading her. "But, that's not what *you* think."

Betty gave a half-smile. "I just felt like I had to tell you."

He emitted a deep sigh then, and reached to briefly touch the top of Betty's hand. "Thank you for telling me. The trouble is…"

She titled her head, waiting for him to continue.

He sighed again, in a resigned sort of way. "I have no idea how my parents died."

Betty's jaw dropped slightly.

"I know," he responded. "It seems incomprehensible, doesn't it?"

"How is it that you don't know?"

Thomas closed his eyes briefly. "That is more difficult to answer. Part of it is that my cousins, the Erwinshires, never told me. The other part of it is that I never asked. You see," he continued, "I was taken in by them when I was not

yet a year old. They *were—are*—my family. I always looked
to them as parents, and my cousins as brothers and sisters.
And, in fact, I didn't know any different until I was eleven or
twelve years old."

He gave a short laugh. "It was by happenstance,
actually." He went on to explain in response to her inquiring
expression. "I had some school project or other—the one
where you draw your parents and write down some facts
about them—"

Betty nodded in understanding.

"I asked permission to bring my project home so that I
could get some facts about my parents. Of course, that was
fine. So, I go home that day, tell my family about it, and I
remember that my Aunt Violet had this odd look on her face.
And then she said something like, 'it's time we told you about
your parents.'"

Betty looked at him with a mix of sadness and empathy.
"How strange that must have been for you."

"That's one way to describe it," he replied, shaking his
head as if in continued disbelief of what had occurred on that
day. "The other funny thing is, I had always called my aunt
and uncle by their first names, 'Violet and Robert.' All of us
did. I guess that should have tipped me off, but it didn't."

There was an edge of bitterness in his voice. Betty well
understood the complicated emotions attached to names and
identity through the secret of her name; but even at that, she
knew that her feelings could not compare to his in this
situation.

"They sat me down and we started to have the
conversation. I don't remember all that was said, honestly,
but I do remember how I *felt*." He paused for a moment, and
it seemed like the feelings were flooding back to him as he sat
there in the café. "It was confusing, and a little sad, and I was

scared—scared for the first time about who I was and where I belonged. But they were kind about it, and loving. I eventually accepted it, though still considered them my parents even after I learned that they were really my aunt and cousins."

"What...what did...." Betty spoke tentatively, and Thomas nodded to indicate that it was okay for her to ask a question. "What did they actually tell you about your parents?"

"That they had gone away, through no fault of their own, and were not coming back."

Betty frowned and asked, "And did you accept that?"

"As odd as it sounds, yes I did," he admitted. "I was very young then, even for an eleven-year-old. And I suppose I just took everything Violet and Robert said as the truth, and didn't question it." He looked about the room, as if searching for the things he did not say then, but wanted to say now. "I never even asked what had happened to my 'real' parents, or why they were not coming back."

He returned his gaze to Betty. "I think that I didn't want to know. And, after that, things went back to normal and we all kind of...forgot about it."

Betty studied him. "But, at some point, you began to feel differently."

"A few years ago, I found that school project, and it all came flooding back. I reminded Violet about it, and I *did* ask her what had happened to my parents. Maybe a part of me wanted to find them and visit them." He paused again, and drew a hand across his brow. "Then she told me that they had died."

Betty could tell that the weight of his Aunt's admission still affected him.

"I think I was angry then," he continued. "And I asked

her how it happened, but she said she didn't know, or couldn't tell me, or..." he struggled as he recalled the memory. "Then...then she gave me this." He let out a soft breath and gestured towards the notepad with the lines of the poem written on it. "She gave me a copy of the poem, and several photographs. Remnants of *her*—my mother. I have cherished them ever since."

Betty could not find any words that would be sufficient. She sighed, and felt a teardrop upon her cheek as she drew a fingertip across the lines of the poem on the table in front of her.

"And then I met you," Thomas said softly. "And it's all coming back."

Betty glanced up and brushed the dampness from her face. "For that, I must apologize."

"No, no, that's not cause for an apology," he said emphatically. "With you—the poem—this town—I feel closer, more connected to my mother and to myself."

Betty looked at him with surprise.

"It is something to be glad about, I promise you. I feel closer to the truth, finally, and it is because of you."

Betty smiled and shook her head. "If this has truly made you feel that way, then I *am* glad about it. But I have done nothing."

Thomas looked as though he wanted to say something else to her, but could not quite come up with the right words to express his thoughts. Somehow, Betty knew that it had to do with her connection to the Sebastian poem, and she filled the silent space by saying, "Your mother's poem always held a certain power."

The corners of Thomas' lips lifted, and he said, "That must be it. In an odd way, I feel the poem is pulling me towards her."

Betty smiled, and the heaviness in the atmosphere with their earlier conversation lifted and gave way to easiness.

She leaned her face in her hands, and said, in a contemplative way, "So, you really don't know how your parents passed?"

He leaned back and shook his head. "But assuming there *is* some connection between me and Mrs. Highley's 'Thomas E.', then we have a clue there."

"Hmm," Betty responded, nodding slowly.

"Any chance we can get more information about that carriage accident?" he asked.

Betty leaned back herself, and said, "As a matter of fact, there is. I've had a telegram from Mrs. Highley since the party, and she may have a letter that can shed some light. I'll talk with her about it."

Thomas nodded, and then glanced at his timepiece with a look of surprise on his face. "But not tonight. Goodness, would you look at the time! I'm so sorry, I've kept you far too late." He immediately stood up from his chair and walked around the table to help Betty out of her own chair.

She shot him an amused look at his hurry to depart. "I'm afraid it is *I* who kept *you* with all of my questions."

He helped her with her coat and held her notepad as she gathered up her shoulder bag. "The fault is equal, then. Either way, I need to get you and Leopold home. Is your mother a stickler on time?"

In a few minutes, they gathered their belongings, bid goodnight to the host, and stepped out into the evening air. The clocktower showed eight-o-clock. Thomas seemed worried, and asked if Betty was warm enough several times as they walked back the way they came. Betty sought to ease him by saying that she had let her mother know she would be out this evening; that it was unlikely her mother would be waiting up for them; and that it was not so late, in any case. This, however, did little to ease Thomas, and he continued on at a brisk pace until Betty urged him to wait for Leopold to catch up with them.

They arrived at the Featherwin home soon enough. Thomas escorted Betty and Leopold to the door, and handed the manuscript and notepad back to Betty.

"Oh, we never did discuss the manuscript," she said, as she took them. "And I never asked where you're staying, and for how long. Do you want to look over my questions?" she continued in a rush.

He chuckled. "Certainly not, and rest easy. I'm staying at the inn again, and although I can't say for sure how long I'll stay, I expect it will be for a little while longer."

Betty smiled at this, and they stood together on the porch for a moment until she said, "Next week. Come by the shop then, won't you?"

"Of course," he responded, and then stepped back a pace and dipped his head in his usual way of greeting. "Good night, Ms. Featherwin."

"Good night," she replied, and the two parted, Thomas pausing to make sure she got into the house all right before turning up the road to go to the local inn. As Betty entered, with Leopold scampering ahead of her and going in the direction of her room, she leaned against the front door with a sigh. What an eventful couple of weeks it had been, and what the following week had in store, she could only imagine.

Chapter 13
T.Y.L.

After a drowsy and rainy weekend, the new week signaled a mid-August rush of revelations for several people in Coos County. Mrs. Martha Mabel, the suffragist who attended Mrs. Highley's Saturday tea, had made it up to Portland and sent a telegram to every woman in town with a plea to join her in solidarity. It was unclear whether anyone answered her, but, in any case, Martha was far too preoccupied to care. A picture turned up in the newspapers, showing Martha in between a group of women, captioned, *Suffragists Gather to Celebrate National Victory.*[6] It seemed that Martha had found her calling. Meanwhile, Edith Smithson had been seen about town more frequently with her beau, Samuel, and rumors began to fly about their engagement.

Betty was too absorbed in her own revelations to give a second thought to Martha or Edith. The weekend felt longer than usual after the time she spent with Thomas on Friday, learning much more than she had anticipated. When Bea asked after her evening, Betty described it as pleasant but did not go into any details. Bea did not pry, and went on with her cooking and embroidery to fill the time inside due to the inclement weather. Betty meanwhile spent a good deal of time thinking over what Thomas had said regarding his parents as she sat at the windowpane with Leopold, watching the rain fall. She also continued to think about the Sebastian poem, and took the envelope containing the card out of her

---

[6] This references actual news articles from August 1920: "Suffragists Here Celebrate Victory," *Sunday Oregonian*, August 29, 1920 and "Suffrage Leaders of Portland Gather at Hotel to Celebrate National Victory," *Sunday Oregonian*, August 29, 1920.

nightstand. The card, of course, had an entirely new meaning now. The lines of poetry written on it were not just the words of a poem she enjoyed; they were the words of Thomas' mother. As she thought this, a shiver ran through her that had nothing to do with the chill in the air. It was peculiar how Thomas had stayed connected to his mother through the poem, and then became drawn into the literary world himself. This was similar to how Betty stayed connected to her father through The Sapphire Key, she supposed. The realization was astounding to her, but, in a strange way, it helped her to understand things more clearly than ever before.

Betty felt differently about Leopold too. He was a part of the family now, and had made his home in the town as much as he had made it in The Sapphire Key and in the Featherwin house. The locals were all used to the large orange cat. They expected to see him on their walks and during their visits to The Sapphire Key. People also expected to see Betty and Leopold together. It was no longer a surprise to see the pair walking side-by-side at the pier, or sitting next to one another in the church pew. It was clear that the young woman and the cat had a bond that seemed to grow only stronger. It was hard for Betty to believe that she had met the cat just several months ago, and now could not imagine her days without him.

He was still very communicative with her. Ever since the night when he brought Betty her misplaced keys, she felt that he could understand her. Likewise, she could easily pick up on his moods through the tone and quality of his vocalizations. His facial features, and especially his eyes, were very expressive as well. To Betty, his eyes appeared a brighter shade of green when he was happy or excited about something, and turned softer and darker at other times. She also noticed the way his ears and whiskers twitched when she was speaking to him, as if he were truly listening and reacting to her words. She told herself that she could just be imagining it, but could not deny the connection between herself and the cat. No one else had picked up on it, and Betty preferred to keep it that way. Just like her full name was her secret, her unique bond with Leopold would be her secret too.

***

The one thing she did not want to remain a secret, however, was the truth about Thomas' parents. Thomas did not want to be shielded from the truth anymore either.

They found an opportunity to talk on Monday afternoon during lunch. Thomas, it turned out, had engaged in much reflecting over the weekend as well. He told Betty that their conversation had renewed his interest in learning more about his parents, and he was determined to get to the bottom of it. His cousins were a dead end, unfortunately. He did not expect to get any more information from Violet, and no one else seemed to know anything about his parents. Either that, or they were just unwilling to share what they knew.

Although it was a longshot, Thomas and Betty agreed that the story of "Thomas E. and the carriage accident" from the Highley tea could lead to some answers. Betty was therefore hopeful about her impending visit from Mrs. Highley. After lunch with Thomas, she sent a return telegram to her, suggesting Tuesday or Wednesday afternoon for her visit. On Thursday, however, Betty still had not received a response confirming the visit, and began to feel concerned. It was unlike Mrs. Highley to forget an appointment. She later found out that her niece, May, had decided to extend her stay in town and Mrs. Highley had been busy at home. Betty understood this, of course, but felt disappointed nonetheless.

With Mrs. Highley's visit on hold, Betty and Thomas

placed their conversations about Thomas' parents on hold too. In the interim, they occupied themselves with the large task of reviewing the manuscript, and discussing the publication and distribution details. Thomas told Betty about the author, Theodore Yousef Lamore (or, T.Y.L.), who was up-and-coming in sports fiction. He had written several magazine articles about baseball, which received positive reviews. Taking this as encouragement, he then started on his draft of fiction. Thomas' associate found out about him through a friend of a friend, and after some initial interviews, felt that T.Y.L.'s manuscript would be a good fit for Erwinshire Publishing. The manuscript was then passed on to Thomas, who placed a call to T.Y.L. and found him remarkably likeable.

"His phone etiquette was superb," Thomas told Betty. "I thought, if he can pull off a telephone interview with that much confidence, then he can pull off a best-selling book."

Betty laughed at this and remarked, "Well, he did not disappoint."

The publication process would take another couple of months to complete, Thomas explained. The books needed to be printed and bounded, and the contract terms settled between T.Y.L. and Erwinshire Publishing. Then, the books would be sent out to any distributors. These distributors contracted with Erwinshire Publishing on terms under which distributors showcased the book in their stores for sale, and received a commission for books sold. These terms were standard, and Betty was quite familiar with them based on her arrangements with other publishers over the years. She was comforted that Erwinshire Publishing followed the same standards. She also appreciated that Thomas cared about the quality of books that he endorsed. All in all, it seemed like a good fit.

With this decided, Betty and Thomas discussed how to handle the manuscript edits and mark-ups. Betty assumed that Thomas would handle the edits himself, and asked if he would like to take the manuscript back to his room at the inn to finish up the work. He was down on this suggestion, however, stating that he was impressed by Betty's comments and would not mind working with her on it, if she was amenable. Surprised and flattered, Betty accepted this proposition, and they spent the next couple of weeks working together to make notes and corrections on the manuscript.

Betty enjoyed seeing Thomas' editing process. Unlike Betty (who often thought and wrote in silence), Thomas was a vocal editor. That is, he preferred to dictate his edits and paced the room while doing so. He was also meticulous, and could notice the slightest spelling error or misplaced punctuation. This type of editing took longer, but resulted in a cleaner and more complete manuscript.

To accommodate this type of work, Thomas came over to the Reading Room in the Sapphire Key in the late afternoon or early evening. There, they had ample room to set out the manuscript pages and were out-of-the-way and apart from the rest of the bookshop. The Reading Room, being enclosed as a separate room, also ensured that they would not be disturbed in their work. It was a good arrangement for them, and even Leopold agreed. As they worked, he liked to lounge in front of the hearth and fall asleep to the sound of their voices. It was a pleasant picture—the three working away in the later hours of the day in a room designed for it, the rain pattering against the large window all the while.

This continued each work day for two weeks, and they all (Betty, Leopold, and Elizabeth) became rather used to Thomas. He was slowly getting to know some others in town. Actually, the locals started to ask about "the new gentleman frequenting The Sapphire Key." He was being noticed. Because of this, Betty wondered if she would receive an invitation to a luncheon soon, with a request to bring Mr. Thomas Erwinshire as a guest. Coos County, particularly Marshfield and North Bend, was a tight-knit community, and newcomers were obvious from a mile away. If Thomas remained in Marshfield any longer, Betty surmised, they would certainly receive an invitation so that Thomas could be introduced properly. She pondered, as they worked together on the manuscript, how long he would remain in Marshfield. He had said "a little while longer." The thought of him returning to Washington saddened her, to her surprise, and so she decided to put off asking him. She would ask after they had finished the work on the manuscript.

✳✳✳

The more time Thomas spent at The Sapphire Key meant that Leopold was getting used to him as well. Leopold liked nearly everyone, but was only really attached to Betty. Lately, though, Betty had noticed Leopold staying near Thomas when he came into the shop and becoming quite talkative. Betty was accustomed to this behavior, as Leopold usually meowed and vocalized with her. However, he did not usually do this with anyone else.

This was fine, and Thomas did not seem to mind. The only thing that concerned Betty was Thomas' comments one evening. He had come into The Sapphire Key just before closing. Betty was already in the Reading Room, organizing her papers across the table and turning on all of the lamps so that the room would be well-lit. Leopold was there with her, and they were having what Betty could only describe as a conversation. As she tidied up, she made casual remarks to Leopold about the day's events. Leopold followed her about the room and meowed in response. It was quite normal to her, but a stranger might have considered the scene odd. Thomas entered the room as she and Leopold were going back and forth, and Betty was startled when he cleared his throat and interrupted them.

"Hello. I didn't mean to disturb your conversation."

He was pleasant as usual, his tone of voice was kind, and he did not mention anything else about it. Still, Betty wondered what Thomas thought when he walked in to hear Betty talking to Leopold, and the cat talking back in his own meowing way.

✳✳✳

The two weeks of work on the manuscript came to an end quicker than either Betty or Thomas anticipated. For the first time since she had met him, Betty was at a true loss for words. At length, Thomas was the first to speak. It was a quarter until eight, and they stood outside in front of the Featherwin house, Thomas having accompanied Betty and Leopold on the walk home from The Sapphire Key.

"I want to thank you, for all of your time and help," he said with sincerity, and then sighed as he looked at her. "*Thank you* is nowhere near sufficient, but I do mean it."

"You're welcome," she replied. "This time has been…" She paused and found it difficult to say the right word, but he seemed to understand her meaning and nodded. She finally asked the question that she had been putting off. "When do you return to Washington?"

"Well, I hadn't set a firm date. But, now that the manuscript is ready, my associate will be expecting me back. He's been holding the fort since I've been away, which is *not* his style. He's likely chomping at the bit to be relieved." Thomas' voice was light, but there was a note of reluctance in it.

Betty recalled that Thomas' associate traveled and rarely was in the office. Everything Thomas said made sense, and it was right for him to go back. The fact was, she did not want him to go.

Betty just looked down at the keys in her hands and said, "That makes perfect sense, and of course you should make arrangements."

Thomas was silent for a moment, and then responded, "All right. Perhaps…perhaps I'll come back."

Betty looked up at him then, wanting to say the words on the tip of her tongue, but feeling restrained from doing so.

"For the book showcase, just to make sure everything is good to go."

"Oh." Betty closed her eyes and nodded. "Yes, of course. Is…is there any chance you might come back before then?" she asked cautiously.

He smiled then, and pressed her hand briefly. "If there *is* a chance, then I will. Most definitely."

As he released her hand, she remembered something that they had dismissed while working on the manuscript. "I'm glad we accomplished so much with the manuscript. But I am sorry we couldn't learn more about your parents."

"Oh," he sighed. "That nearly slipped my mind. It's all right. We tried, but maybe I'm not meant to learn more."

She frowned then, and said, "I *don't* believe that is true."

His soft laugh surprised her. "Well, I believe in your faith, Betty. If there is an answer to find, I know that you'll find it."

She gave a wry smile. "I'm not so sure of that. And, anyway, *we* were supposed to find the answer."

"Hmm," he nodded, and then said, after a moment of reflection, "You do have my address and telephone number. Contact me, if you like. And, if it's all right, I'll drop you a line every now and again."

She smiled. "I would not only *like* it; I *expect* it, Mr. Erwinshire."

He returned the smile. "Then I will write to you."

There was a few moments' pause, as if neither of them knew what else to say though remained reluctant to part. It was Leopold's meow that interrupted the pause.

Thomas looked down at the cat, who gazed back at him with bright eyes. "Betty, I'd like to see you again, before I leave."

"I'd like that too," she responded quickly.

Thomas sighed in what sounded like an audible expression of relief. "How about tomorrow for lunch, if your schedule allows?"

"That's perfect," she answered, feeling gladdened, at least, at the prospect of having a proper goodbye.

"Good," he responded, confirming the plan, and then dipped his head. "Then I'll bid you good night, and see you tomorrow."

Betty started to watch him turn away, but then called out to stop him. "Thomas—wait."

He turned back to her, creasing his brow in puzzlement as he watched her take something out of her shoulder bag. It was a small white envelope.

"Here," she said, and handed the envelope to him. "This is your bookmark. I've been meaning to give it back to you."

He looked at the outside of the envelope, and the words *M.B. Sebastian* in Betty's handwriting, and then opened it. He drew in a breath as he held the card in his fingers. Then, a gaze passed between them at the remembrance of their conversation at the café when they realized what the poem meant to both of them.

"Betty, I…" he started to say, but halted when he saw

the porch lights flicker on. A voice sounded from inside and then the front door opened.

Bea Featherwin stood there in the doorway, calling out, "Betty, I thought I heard you out here. What are you—oh, I see you have company?"

Betty, who had startled at Bea's voice, cleared her throat and said, "Mother, this is Mr. Thomas Erwinshire, the publisher. And…" she glanced at Thomas. "This is Beatrice, my mother."

"Oh," Bea said in realization. "It's a pleasure to meet you, Mr. Erwinshire. Betty has spoken about you."

Thomas bowed to her. "The pleasure is mine, Mrs. Featherwin. It is an honor to meet you."

Bea smiled, looking from Betty to Thomas. "Well, would you like to come in, Mr. Erwinshire? I've just put on some tea."

"No—thank you," he responded. "I just wanted to see your daughter home safely. Now I'll take my leave, and I wish you a good night."

They exchanged "good nights" in a rather hurried way, and then Thomas turned to go on his way to the inn. Bea and Betty went inside, and Betty remained quiet as she slipped off her coat and placed it on the coatrack in the parlor.

"Betty," Bea called, and Betty looked up at her. "You should invite that young man for tea."

Betty sighed and murmured, "I can't."

"And why ever not?"

"Because he's leaving and I don't know when he'll be back," Betty answered, and then turned down the hall towards her room, suddenly not in the mood for tea. When she reached her room, she collapsed into her rocking chair, feeling as though it were very late and she was very tired.

Chapter 14
The Photograph

The following morning dawned bright and sunny. Betty was awoken by sunlight which streamed through her window and the sound of Leopold's purr. She sat up and stroked the soft fur on Leopold's back, thinking about the day ahead. It was an odd feeling that settled in her chest, and she could not quite understand it. She was not sure if she was looking forward to the day or dreading it. Either way, she had to rise and face it.

"Time to get up," she said to the cat. "If we say goodbye to one thing, we say hello to another," she continued, more to reassure herself than to make conversation.

Bea was cheery once Betty stepped into the kitchen, supplying her with a scone and a cup of tea. Kindly, Bea did not remark on what had occurred last night and did not mention Thomas. She merely wished Betty a good day, and, as Betty was on her way out, she said, "Oh, and I meant to tell you that Alice Highley paid me a visit yesterday."

Betty paused in putting on her coat and turned back around. "She did? What did she say?"

"We had some tea and chatted for just a bit. She's had an excellent crop of strawberries and wondered if I could use any for marmalade."

"Oh," Betty replied, her shoulders dropping.

"She also mentioned coming by the bookshop to bring you something. She didn't mention what it is."

Betty's spirits lifted. "Oh! Well, did she say when she's coming?"

"She said she might try to pop over today," Bea replied.

"What?" Betty exclaimed. "Why didn't you tell me

sooner?"

"Well," Bea responded with a slight frown. "I would have told you last night, but you didn't seem to be in the mood."

Betty returned to her and placed a kiss on her cheek. "Thanks for telling me. And now I must be off."

Without giving Bea a chance to reply, Betty ran out the door, Leopold at her heels, and felt a bit brighter about the day ahead.

***

The morning hours passed at a steady clip. There was a note from Elizabeth, left from the prior evening, that she would be late today. Betty did not mind, as the workload was light and the number of customers manageable. The pre-luncheon rush began a little earlier than usual, and in the flurry of customers, Betty spotted Mrs. Highley. She was glad that she had been expecting her. Smiling and waving, she indicated that Mrs. Highley should take a seat at the front counter. After assisting a customer with finding a book in the History section of the shop, she was able to break away and join her.

"Mrs. Highley," she greeted, and stepped forward to embrace her. "I'm glad you've come."

"Hello, dear," she responded. "I hope this is not a bad time; I can see that you're busy. I did tell your mother that I might come by today. Did she—?"

"Oh yes, mother let me know. Now is perfect. If I need to assist a customer, then I will. But for now, I'm happy to talk to you. Tell me, what's new?"

"Well, thank you, first of all. I never did respond to your note on time, which was bad manners."

Betty shook her head, murmuring, "No problem at all."

"Still, I appreciate your flexibility. With May and

Florence here a bit longer than expected, there was a lot to do."

"I trust they've made it back home safely."

"Yes, they have. And Florence said to tell you that she enjoyed meeting Leopold."

Betty smiled.

"But that's not the reason I'm here," Mrs. Highley continued. "I did not forget our conversation from a few weeks ago. I promised you that I would find a letter written by my sister, Sarah."

Betty felt her heart lift. This is what she had been waiting and hoping for. She could scarcely wait to find out what was in the letter. What information would there be about Thomas E. and the carriage accident?

"I'm afraid I wasn't able to find it," Mrs. Highley said. Betty felt her heart begin to drop again, until Mrs. Highley continued, "But I found this instead."

She reached into her handbag and took out a worn and faded photograph. The edges were slightly torn, and there was a crease down the middle, as if it had been folded in half more than once. Clearly visible, though, were the two women standing together who had been the subject of the photograph. One was tall and full-figured, with soft dark eyes that seemed to peer straight out of the photo. The other was slighter in stature, in a long, floor-length dress with heavy lace at the collar. Both women wore hats and gloves, and looked to be similar in age. The smaller of the two had a parasol in her left hand. Betty studied the photograph, but did not recognize the women.

She looked up at Mrs. Highley, who said, in response to Betty's unspoken question, "The woman on the left is my sister, Sarah. The one on the right is a woman named May. Turn the photograph over and look."

Betty did as she was asked, and flipped the photograph. On the back was written, in faded cursive ink, *Me and May, 1890.* She felt her heart begin to hammer. *May, 1890.* She turned the photograph back over to study the women again.

"This has nothing to do with what you asked me, and maybe it doesn't interest you," Mrs. Highley was saying. "But as I was looking through my boxes, I found this and something told me to show it to you."

After looking at the photograph a moment longer, Betty returned her gaze to Mrs. Highley and replied, "I'm so glad you did."

Mrs. Highley gave her an inquiring look. "I think it *does* interest you. Is this photograph familiar to you?"

"No—yes—well, only…" she stammered, and then collected herself. "Only, this may be familiar to a friend. Would you mind if I held onto this, just for today?"

Mrs. Highley raised an eyebrow at this request, but conceded. "No, I don't mind."

"I'll return it to you tomorrow," she promised.

Mrs. Highley nodded dismissively, and then rose out of her chair. "I'm sorry if I can't be of more help." Straightening her hat, she began walking to the shopfront door, and paused when she reached it. Looking at Betty, she said, "Let me know if you or your mother need anything. And I expect to see you both at the next Saturday tea."

Betty smiled as she waved her goodbye. "We wouldn't miss it."

With a final wave, Mrs. Highley stepped out in a soft rustle of her skirts, and the faint scent of her gardenia perfume lingering in the air after her.

✳✳✳

The last of the pre-luncheon customers left the shop at a quarter after twelve. As the shop emptied out, Betty let out a breath. Slipping her hand inside of her front pocket, she felt the edge of the photograph. She took a moment to glance at it again. *Sarah apparently knew the mother, though I never got her name...*Mrs. Highley had said during the Saturday tea. The more that Betty looked at the photograph, the more she wondered if the woman standing next to Sarah Mitchell (Mrs. Alice Highley's sister), was, in any way, connected to Thomas E. and the carriage accident.

The door to the shop jangled, and Betty looked up to see her welcome and expected visitor. There was only one way to find out.

"Betty—"

"Thomas—"

They greeted one another at the same time, and then smiled, glad to see each other. Thomas removed his charcoal gray hat, and fiddled with it. His breath was quick, as if he had been walking fast.

"Betty," he started, "About last night. I wanted to—"

"Wait," she interrupted. "Don't say anything yet. There's something I have to show you."

Creasing his brow, Thomas nonetheless obliged and joined her at the counter. Betty held the photograph in her hands, and then said, "I had a visit from Mrs. Alice Highley today."

"Oh, yes?"

Betty nodded. "She gave me this," she continued, indicating the photograph. "I thought you should see it." She handed it over to Thomas, who looked puzzled momentarily before a flicker of recognition shown on his face.

"What is it?" Betty whispered, as Thomas continued to study the photograph with the same interest that Betty had demonstrated only moments before.

"This...this is incredible," he murmured. He glanced at

Betty, and placed the photograph atop the counter. He gestured for her to stand nearer to look at it. "This woman here," he said, pointing to the small, slight figure with the parasol in her hand, "This is my mother."

Betty felt her heart lift. "Are you…are you sure?" she asked.

"Yes," he replied. "I'm very sure. I have other photos, and this is definitely her." He looked at Betty, surely seeing her changed expression. "But why did Mrs. Highley have this? Who is the other woman in the photo?"

"The other woman," Betty replied slowly, "is Mrs. Highley's sister. If your mother is standing beside her, then—"

"Then Mrs. Highley's sister and my mother knew each other," Thomas finished the sentence, a sense of realization dawning over him. He looked at the photograph again with renewed understanding.

"My God."

Betty simply nodded and then replied, "And you'll see the date on the back, it's 1890."

Thomas turned the photograph over as she spoke. "1890. Why, that's some years before I was born. She may not have even met my father yet."

The two looked at one another for a quiet moment. As they stood, considering this newfound knowledge, they felt that the world had shifted and realigned to make sense of things that did not make sense before. It was Thomas who broke the silence.

He said softly, "It wasn't *you* who found the answer."

To her perplexed look, he continued, "You were right. *We* were supposed to find the answer, together."

Betty smiled broadly. "We haven't quite found anything yet."

"No," he replied, "But we have a good start." He returned the smile then, and it was a smile that could be seen in his hazel eyes.

Betty swallowed. "Does this mean…"

Thomas nodded, and a ripple of understanding passed between them. They knew then that Thomas would indeed be staying in Coos County, as long as he could convince his associate to hold down the fort at the office for a little while longer. He also wished to speak to Mrs. Highley himself. Perhaps she would remember something more.

***

As the three of them—Betty, Thomas, and Leopold—left the shop to go to lunch at the café near the pier, Betty asked Thomas what he wanted to tell her when he came into the shop. He told her that he had forgotten. It did not quite matter, really. He had wanted to tell her that he changed his mind about leaving and instead planned to extend his stay. Now, he had even more reason to stay and it did not require an explanation. He would tell her one day, during a long train ride together spent reminiscing about an afternoon in August of 1920. For now, though, all thoughts were on the future, and they would be spending their lunch—the three of them—making plans for what would happen next. Betty had become somewhat comfortable with the secret of her unfortunate first name and her very communicative cat. Now, a third secret had been placed into her lap.

The End

Afterword

While this book is a work of fiction, and the scenes, characters and events are a product of my imagination, the setting and historical references throughout the book are based in reality. Coos County, where this story takes place, is a real-life region on the southern coast of Oregon. Locales like the North Bend Mill & Lumber Company, the pier, and the estate of Louis J. Simpson, did, in fact, exist in 1920. A few of my distant family members found their way to Coos County in the 1800s and 1900s, and worked on the railroad, which was a booming industry during that time. It was an interesting, rich life for them. There was so much newness coming into the world—the telephone, advances in transportation, and changes in the political and social atmosphere—but the area retained its history and charm. As an homage to them, and to that captivating time, I drew from this historical setting to create the world of Betty Featherwin, her friends, and her family.

About the Author

Sarah Jane Gross has spent a good portion of her life on a college campus. After graduating from high school, she lived on campus at the University of California, Davis in northern California, where she graduated with a Bachelor's in English and Expository Writing. After graduation, she stayed on to receive a teaching credential and Master's in Education and, for a while, taught middle school and high school English. She then pursued further education, and attended Chapman University School of Law in southern California, where she graduated with a law degree. After passing the Bar exam, she worked for a firm practicing education law. She then decided to focus on a different area of law, and was accepted to Pepperdine University School of Law in the coastal city of Malibu, California in Los Angeles County. She lived on campus and graduated with a Master's in Law through the Straus Institute for Dispute Resolution. She returned to Orange County, where she spearheaded a pilot program in eldercaring coordination for the courts. She continues to advocate for court-connected programs to address the needs of elders and their families, including mediation programs. Sarah has had many legal articles published, and enjoys creative writing, which has always been a passion for her.

***

Coming Soon...

Be sure to purchase Book 2 to continue this journey with Betty Featherwin.